BAT
and the End of Everything

WRITTEN BY
Elana K. Arnold

WITH PICTURES BY
Charles Santoso

WALDEN POND PRESS
An Imprint of HarperCollinsPublishers

Bat and the End of Everything
Text copyright © 2019 by Elana K. Arnold
Illustrations copyright © 2019 by Charles Santoso
All rights reserved. Printed in the United States of America.
No part of this book may be used or reproduced in any manner
whatsoever without written permission except in the case of brief
quotations embodied in critical articles and reviews. For information
address HarperCollins Children's Books, a division of HarperCollins
Publishers, 195 Broadway, New York, NY 10007.
www.harpercollinschildrens.com

Library of Congress Cataloging-in-Publication Data

Names: Arnold, Elana K., author. | Santoso, Charles, illustrator.
Title: Bat and the end of everything / written by Elana K. Arnold ;
    with pictures by Charles Santoso.
Description: First edition. | New York, NY: Walden Pond Press, an
    imprint of HarperCollinsPublishers, [2019] |
Summary: "Bat grows anxious as his third-grade year comes to an
    end and the time to release his pet skunk, Thor, out into the
    wild approaches."—Provided by publisher.
Identifiers: LCCN 2018025430 | ISBN 978-0-06-279845-9 (paperback)
Subjects: | CYAC: Autism—Fiction. | Skunks as pets—Fiction. |
    Wildlife rehabilitation—Fiction. | Family life—Fiction.
Classification: LCC PZ7.A73517 Bat 2019 | DDC [Fic]—dc23 LC
    record available at https://lccn.loc.gov/2018025430

Typography by Aurora Parlagreco
20 21 22 23 24   PC/BRR   10 9 8 7 6 5 4 3 2 1
❖
First paperback edition, 2020

For Joe, Sam, Oliver, and Henry, My Niblings,
with Love

Contents

1. An Offer   1

2. A Perfect Plan   8

3. In the Back Seat   14

4. In the Kitchen   20

5. Ezra's House   26

6. A Gift for Thor   33

7. An Idea   41

8. To Jenny, From Bat   46

9. Under the Play Structure   53

10. The Last Day of Third Grade   59

11. Pizza Night   67

12. Doughnuts for Breakfast   74

13. Planning for the Future   81

14. An Assistant's Assistant   89

15. Head Tilt and Snuffles   96

16. House Call   105

17. At the Pool   116

18. Photo Shoot   124

19. Mail Day   131

20. A Hot, Sweaty Day   141

21. Two Parts   152

22. Pancake Juggling   158

23. Family Meeting   168

Author's Note   181

Acknowledgments   183

CHAPTER 1
An Offer

How do you say good-bye to a friend?

That's what Bixby Alexander Tam (known to everyone as Bat) was thinking about, sitting with Babycakes, the class rabbit, in the pen at the back of Mr. Grayson's class. It was the first Monday in June. In four days, the school year would end, and Bat would have to say good-bye.

Right now, he let his eyes go sort of blurry, and

he concentrated on the way Babycakes's fluffy white fur felt between his fingers, the reassuring softness of it. He could feel Babycakes breathing in and out. He could see Babycakes's body expand and contract with each breath.

Babycakes was content, sitting in the small diamond of space between Bat's crisscrossed legs. The rabbit trusted Bat. The rabbit knew that Bat would never hurt her.

Outside of the pen, the classroom was quiet. Bat had wanted to get to school early this morning, so it was just him and Babycakes and, of course, Mr. Grayson.

There was Mr. Grayson, sitting behind his desk. He wasn't grading papers or writing notes about the day or doing anything, as far as Bat could tell. He was just sitting there, his elbows on his desk, his chin resting on the palms of his hands, watching Bat and Babycakes. His arms wore an assortment of colorful bracelets, and he had an orange bandanna wrapped around his right wrist.

Bat looked back down at the rabbit. He wondered how long Babycakes would be comfortable sitting right there, just like that, if nothing came along to interrupt them. Eventually, Babycakes would get hungry or would have to go to the bathroom. Eventually, she would have to move.

But Bat wished that they could stay just like that, with Babycakes tucked into the hollow of his lap, with Mr. Grayson peacefully watching them.

"Are you sure you won't reconsider?" Mr. Grayson asked.

Bat was quiet. He knew what Mr. Grayson was talking about; just five minutes earlier, he had asked Bat if he would like to bring Babycakes home for the summer and take care of her until school started again in the fall.

Under normal circumstances, there would have

been only one answer for a question like that: Yes!

But circumstances weren't that simple. Not anymore. Not since Bat had become the caretaker of Thor, the orphaned skunk kit his mom had rescued and brought home until he was ready to be released into the wild.

"I already asked your mom, and she said it would be okay with her," Mr. Grayson said.

Even though Bat loved Babycakes, and even though he would love to have Babycakes live at his house all summer long—with him and his mom and his older sister, Janie, and Thor, the skunk kit—he shook his head.

"Thor needs me," he said. "And I don't know if I can be the best skunk caretaker *and* the best rabbit caretaker at the same time."

Mr. Grayson pushed back his chair and stood. Bat heard the familiar squeak of Mr. Grayson's high-top sneakers as he walked to the back of the classroom, and he knew, when the squeaking stopped, that Mr. Grayson was near the rabbit pen, even though Bat was once again staring down with blurry eyes at Babycakes's soft white fluff.

Mr. Grayson knelt down so that he was right next to Bat, just on the other side of the pen. "Bat,"

5

he said, "you know, summer is almost here, and pretty soon it's going to be time to release Thor. And I thought—well, your mom and I *both* thought that maybe having Babycakes around could help make it easier for you, when the time comes to say good-bye."

There was that word again, the same one Bat had been thinking about. *Good-bye.*

Bat didn't mean to make a sound. He knew how important it was to be quiet and still if he didn't want Babycakes to hop away. But the sound came out anyway—kind of high-pitched and loud, like a chirp, but sadder.

And Babycakes twitched her ears and jolted away, in one swift hop, out of the shelter of Bat's lap, and with two more hops, into the plastic hutch, until only her fluffy white hindquarters were showing.

"Think about it a little more," Mr. Grayson said. "We can talk about it this week. There's still time."

Bat rocked a little bit, forward and backward, the way he sometimes did when he was feeling overwhelmed. Mr. Grayson said that there was still time . . . but time, Bat felt, was moving much, much too fast.

CHAPTER 2
A Perfect Plan

Soon, the classroom was full of noise and color and smells and movement as Bat's classmates poured inside.

Mei, who sat in the desk to the right of Bat's, smelled like strawberries today.

"You smell like strawberries," Bat said.

"I got a new shampoo," Mei said, smiling. "Do you like it?"

"Yes," said Bat.

"Thank you," said Mei, which was a weird thing to do—to thank someone for liking something.

But Bat knew that what he'd said made Mei happy. "You're welcome."

All around him, kids were laughing and unzipping their backpacks and scraping back their chairs and tapping their pencils. It was the last week of school, after all. Everyone was excited.

Well, almost everyone. Bat was not excited.

Bat did his best to ignore all the activity and movement, to ignore the loud conversation happening behind him between Lucca and Ramon about how hot it was outside, and how they couldn't *wait* for summer, so they could go to the lake and the pool and the movie theater. Bat was focused on the classroom doorway.

He was waiting for Israel.

To make waiting easier, Bat focused on a plan he had come up with just a few minutes ago, after Babycakes had hopped away from him but before the students started rushing into class. It seemed to Bat like a perfect plan. He was sure Israel would agree with him. But if Israel didn't get to class soon, Bat wouldn't have a chance to talk with him before it was time to start math, and then he'd have to wait until recess, and Bat did not want to wait until recess.

Fortunately for Bat, Israel showed up right then. Bat felt relief wash over him, almost exactly as if someone had gently poured a pitcher of perfectly warm water over his back. All his muscles relaxed; his shoulders, which had been hunched up almost to his ears, dropped back down, and his fingers melted flat against the top of his desk.

"Hey, Bat," Israel said as he came up the aisle toward Bat.

"You should take Babycakes home for the summer," Bat said, getting the words out fast so that they would have time to work it all out before Mr. Grayson started class.

Israel flinched a little, like the words were too loud. "Huh?" he said.

"Babycakes needs a caretaker for the summer and it should be you so that I can come over and visit her a lot. You would also be a good rabbit caretaker, and I can help you. Okay? Let's tell Mr. Grayson." And Bat started to get up.

"Whoa," said Israel. "Don't you remember? I'm leaving the day after school ends. I'm going to visit my cousin Robert in Canada. I'll be gone for the whole rest of June and part of July."

Now that Israel mentioned it, Bat *did* remember. Israel had told Bat about the trip last weekend when he'd come over to Bat's house for pizza night. He had told Bat how excited he was to see Robert again, and what a great time they'd had when they'd seen each other two years ago, and how cool Robert was, and how funny Robert was.

"Oh," said Bat. He could feel all his muscles getting tight again. He could feel his shoulders creeping back up toward his ears. "I really wish you weren't leaving."

"Are you going to miss me?" Israel asked.

Bat looked up from the honey-brown top of his desk. He looked at the way Israel's curly hair stuck out all around his head. Bat would miss that.

He looked at the way Israel smiled with all his teeth, leaning forward like he was really waiting for Bat to answer him. Bat would miss that.

He looked at the way Israel's T-shirt was sort of wrinkly, and how it wasn't tucked in. Bat would miss that, too.

Bat didn't want to talk about missing Israel. He didn't want to miss Israel at all. He wanted Israel to be in town this summer . . . and not only because he wanted Israel to take care of Babycakes so that Bat could visit.

"Yes," said Bat. "I am going to miss you. And so is Babycakes."

CHAPTER 3
In the Back Seat

Mom was waiting for Bat when school ended that afternoon, and Thor was waiting for Bat too.

Thor the skunk kit seemed to like the new routine the family had started. In the mornings, Bat fed him and exercised him and petted his coat, which was coming in thick now, black and white, coarse in some places, like his tail, and soft in others, like his round little belly. Then Bat tucked

Thor into the kitty carrier and took him to the car, along with his backpack. Mom and Thor would drive Bat to school, and then Mom and Thor went on to Mom's veterinary clinic, where the little skunk had his very own crate. Bat knew that Thor slept almost the whole day at the clinic, and so Bat made sure that each week Mom took one of Bat's unwashed shirts to tuck into Thor's crate; that way, he would maybe have dreams about Bat.

Then, in the afternoons, Mom packed Thor in his kitty carrier and together they would come to pick Bat up from school.

It worked like this almost every day, but on Every-Other Fridays, Bat's dad picked him up after school and took Bat home to his apartment for the weekend. But at least Dad sometimes agreed to drop by Mom's veterinary clinic, even though it was out of the way, so that Bat could check on

Thor and say good-bye for the weekend.

Today was not an Every-Other Friday, and Bat felt especially glad about that. He felt reassured when the back door of Mom's burgundy station wagon popped open with the same sound it made every time he pulled the handle, and he felt relieved to see Thor's blue-and-black kitty carrier waiting for him in the back seat. Bat climbed into the car and slid into the middle seat. He heard the satisfying click of his seat belt. Then he peered into the carrier. Thor wasn't asleep; his little nose pushed up against the soft black mesh, twitching as if it was excited to smell Bat.

"Hello, little Bat," said Mom from the front seat. She had waited until Bat fastened his seat belt before she pulled away. Mom was a careful driver. Bat appreciated that.

"Hello," Bat said.

As they drove through town toward home, Bat unzipped the top corner of the carrier and pushed his fingers in, enjoying the way Thor sniffed at them, nudging them with his nose.

"How was your day?" Mom asked. She had the air conditioner turned on, and she adjusted one of the vents so that more cool air blew into the back seat. Bat did not like to be hot, and neither did Thor.

"It was okay," Bat said. Thor, finished saying hello, rustled around and curled into a ball in the back of the kitty carrier. Bat left his fingers where they were.

"Just okay?" Mom asked.

"Just okay," Bat answered.

He looked out the window as they drove. Because they lived in a college town, there were always lots of students riding bicycles, some wearing backpacks and helmets, others with baskets stuffed with books. Bat noticed that most of the students were dressed in shorts and T-shirts, and some of them were wearing skirts. Lots of them had on sandals.

Whether he liked it or not, summer was coming. The warm weather, the end of school, even how big Thor was getting—all of it meant that summer was pretty much here already. And there was nothing Bat could do to stop it.

He couldn't make time slow down. He couldn't make Thor stay small. Sitting in the back of Mom's station wagon, being driven home, Bat felt uncomfortably aware of how many things were out of his control.

"What would you like to eat for dinner?" Mom asked. She turned on her blinker and steered them down Plum Lane, their street, toward their house in the middle of the block.

"Macaroni and cheese," Bat said decisively. "And cupcakes for dessert."

"Okay," Mom said. "Maybe you and Janie can make the cupcakes while I work on the macaroni and cheese."

Bat nodded. He felt better. He wished every-thing was as easy to figure out as what to have for dinner.

CHAPTER 4
In the Kitchen

//

"Use the spatula, Bat, not the wooden spoon."

Janie was using her bossy voice, which was okay with Bat, because when it came to baking, Janie *was* the boss. She was good at all of it: cracking the eggs without getting the gooey clear weird stuff all over her fingers, pouring flour without it puffing up in a cloud, whipping the butter and the milk together, pouring the batter into little cups and scraping out almost every last chocolaty bit . . . with a spatula, *not* a wooden spoon.

Bat set the wooden spoon he'd been using into the sink and found his favorite spatula—the pink one, with a plastic pig head on the handle—in the drawer next to the stove. Janie held the mixing bowl up for him while he scraped cupcake-sized lumps of batter into the little paper liners that sat in each of the baking tin's cups. If Bat had had his way, Thor would have been curled on his shoulder, watching him work, the way he perched to watch Bat do his homework. But in the kitchen, it was usually Janie who got her way, not Bat.

And today, she'd said, "If you want to help me with the cupcakes, the Mephitidae has to go back to your room."

Actually, Bat was so pleased that Janie had finally learned how to say "Mephitidae" correctly— "meh-fit-i-day"—that he almost didn't mind taking Thor back to his enclosure.

"I'll bring you a snack later," Bat had told Thor as he'd set him in the playpen-like hexagon in the corner of his room. Thor had yawned lazily and nuzzled into his nest of T-shirts in the corner.

Janie, of course, had watched Bat wash his hands after he'd returned to the kitchen, which was sort of annoying. Bat understood how important clean hands were for baking.

When all the batter had been poured into the tins, Bat pulled open the oven—which he had

preheated to 350 degrees, just as Janie had told him to do—and Janie slid the still-liquid cupcakes inside. Bat closed the oven door, which made a satisfying thud.

"It's okay to close the oven like that this time, because we're only baking cupcakes," Janie said, "but if we were making popovers, it'd be an entirely different story."

"*Of course* it would be different if we were making popovers," Bat said. "We wouldn't be making cupcakes."

"No, Bat, it'd be a different story because popovers collapse if you aren't careful with the oven door. Soufflés, too."

"But we aren't making popovers or soufflés," Bat said. "We're making cupcakes."

Janie sighed and shook her head. "You're right, Bat," she said. "We're making cupcakes."

"Should we start the frosting?" The frosting was Bat's favorite part—sifting together the powdered sugar and the cocoa, creaming the butter, blending in the sugar mixture and the evaporated milk. Licking the beaters.

"Later," Janie said. "When the cupcakes are cooling. I have to run over to Ezra's house to bring him a book from school."

"Did he forget it?" Bat asked.

"No," Janie said. "He's sick, and our teacher asked me to bring it home for him, since we're neighbors." Then Janie said something unusual. "Want to come with me?"

Normally, Janie did not invite Bat with her to go over to Ezra's house. And normally, Bat wouldn't want to go anyway. Ezra was sort of a tease, and one of his favorite people to tease was Bat. And Bat was not a fan of being teased.

But he was still feeling sort of warm and friendly

after baking together with Janie, so instead of saying no, he asked, "Is Ezra contagious?"

"No," said Janie. "He has infected tonsils. I don't think you can catch it unless you kiss him."

Bat had no intention of kissing Ezra. "Okay," he said. "I'll come."

Janie dug through her backpack, which was hanging on the back of a kitchen chair. She set aside a notebook, two schoolbooks, and her digital camera, which she'd gotten for her birthday a few weeks ago and carried almost everywhere. Finally, she found the book she was looking for. Then she said, "Mom, when the timer rings, take out the cupcakes, okay?"

Mom had just finished grating a block of cheese and was scraping it into a pot on the stove to make the sauce for the mac and cheese. "Okay," she said. Then she looked up and smiled at Bat. "See you soon," she said.

CHAPTER 5
Ezra's House

The front porch of Ezra's house was littered with scooters and scooter parts. Looking more closely, Bat saw that there was only one functioning scooter, a red-and-silver one. There were three scooter decks, seven loose wheels in a variety of colors, one black handle, four black rubber hand grips, and a whole bunch of screws and clamps, some of which looked pretty rusty.

"Does all that belong to Ezra?" Bat asked Janie,

who stepped over the one whole scooter, which was lying on its side right in the middle of everything.

"Uh-huh," she said. "Ezra wants to learn to build scooters, so he takes apart old ones that he finds at yard sales and tries to make better ones out of their parts."

"Did he build that one?" Bat asked, pointing to the red scooter.

"No," Janie said. "That one he got for his birthday."

She rang the doorbell. Immediately, a dog began barking from inside the house.

"Pumpkin, *sit*," came a voice from the other side of the door. "Sit down!"

Janie looked over at Bat and smiled. "Remember Pumpkin?"

Bat did. The last time he had been over to Ezra's house was in October, right before Halloween. Ezra's family had just adopted a puppy from the shelter. At five months old, the puppy already weighed over forty pounds. Ezra's mom had said he was almost full-grown, but Bat didn't think so.

"This dog is going to weigh two hundred pounds one day," Bat had told her.

Ezra's mom had laughed. "What an imagination!"

Ezra's mom opened the door. Out poked a huge, slobbery, black-and-tan face.

"Sit!" said Ezra's mom again. Bat had the feeling that she said that word a lot.

The door opened wider. Ezra's mom was gripping Pumpkin's collar tightly, holding him back as he strained to get to Janie.

"Hi, Pumpkin," she said. "Hi, Mrs. Herrera."

"Hi, Janie," Mrs. Herrera said. "Hello, Bat."

"Pumpkin is looking really good!" Bat said.

He held his hand out, palm up, so that Pumpkin could sniff it and say hello. Pumpkin buried his huge black nose in Bat's hand, leaving a slimy wet trail across it.

"Sorry about that," Mrs. Herrera said. She managed to pull Pumpkin back into the house so that she could open the door wide enough for Janie and Bat to slip inside. The front room, Bat noticed, smelled strongly of wet dog.

"Your house smells like a wet dog," Bat said.

"Bat," Janie hissed.

Mrs. Herrera grimaced. Her face looked like she was smelling the wet dog smell too. "Ezra is in his room," she said. "He'll be happy to see you, Janie."

"Come on, Bat," Janie said, and she started down the hallway toward Ezra's room.

"I'll wait here," Bat said. "I want to visit with Pumpkin."

Maybe Janie said something after that, but if she did, Bat didn't really hear it. He was petting Pumpkin's warm, floppy ears.

"What does he weigh now, Mrs. Herrera? Is he up to a hundred pounds yet?"

"Almost a hundred and twenty," she answered. She didn't sound as happy about that as Bat thought she should.

"What a good dog," Bat said. A drop of saliva the size of a quarter splattered on the toe of Mrs. Herrera's shoe.

"He's gotten as big as he's going to get," Mrs. Herrera said.

"Oh, no, not by a long shot," Bat said. He patted

Pumpkin's head. "Mastiffs can grow until they're five years old."

"He's not a purebred," Mrs. Herrera said. Her voice sounded kind of high and tight.

"He might be," Bat said. "You never know."

Bat heard Janie knock at Ezra's door, and a moment later, Ezra opened it, sticking his head out into the hallway. He was wearing pajamas and his hair was wild, like he'd been sleeping.

"Hey, Janie," he said. His voice was rough and scratchy. "It's weird to see you without your camera for a change."

Janie didn't answer, just thrust the book she'd brought in his direction. "Here," she said.

"Thanks," Ezra said, taking the book. He looked over to the living room, where Bat still stood, stroking Pumpkin's ears. The dog groaned contentedly, and Bat scooted his foot out of the way of a stream of saliva. "Hiya, Batty."

"Hi," said Bat.

"Feel better, Ezra," Janie said, and she walked back to Bat.

"Thank you, Janie," Mrs. Herrera said. "It was nice of you to bring the book."

"You're welcome," Janie answered. "Come on, Bat."

"Good-bye, Pumpkin," Bat said.

Then they were back out on the porch. Maybe Mrs. Herrera tripped or something, Bat thought when the door slammed behind them. Or maybe Pumpkin pushed her.

"Bat," said Janie, picking her way back across the porch, over the scooter parts, "sometimes you are so rude."

Rude? How on earth could Janie think that he had been rude? He had only talked about Mrs. Herrera's pet. If anyone was rude, it was Mrs. Herrera. She hadn't asked him once about Thor.

CHAPTER 6
A Gift for Thor

The cupcakes were delicious. Bat popped the final bite of his second cupcake into his mouth.

"You always put just the right amount of frosting on each cupcake," Bat told Janie, chewing.

"Thanks, Bat," Janie said. "That's a really nice compliment."

The three of them were eating dessert out in the backyard, near Thor's Garden, because it was such a nice evening. Janie had her camera out, and she was taking pictures of the garden in between cupcake bites.

Bat had planted the garden with Israel's help, and tending to the vegetables had become part of Bat's evening routine. The garden had started off with just carrots, corn, and kale, but Bat and his mom had found room to add some broccoli and also a pumpkin plant. The pumpkin had been Mom's idea; it wouldn't be ready to harvest until the fall, near Halloween, and Mom thought it would be fun to make a jack-o'-lantern from it. But the pumpkin plant actually made Bat kind of sad; by the time the pumpkin was big enough to carve, this little garden wouldn't be Thor's anymore. Thor would be back in the wild. And he'd never get a chance to see that jack-o'-lantern.

Suddenly the last bite of cupcake didn't taste

as sweet, and a hard lump in Bat's throat made it hard to swallow.

"I think I'll go hang out with Thor for a while," Bat said. He stood up and brushed cupcake crumbs from his lap.

"Do you want company?" Mom asked.

"Thor *is* company," Bat said, and he went inside.

As he walked through the kitchen, toward the hallway that led to his room, he heard Janie say, "Mom, Bat is going to be really sad when Thor isn't around anymore."

Bat pulled the neck of his T-shirt up into his mouth, something he liked to do when he was feeling emotions he didn't like to feel.

Thor was rustling around in his litter box. Bat waited for him to finish, and then he reached over the side of the playpen.

"Hi, little Thor," he cooed as he reached inside. It was always best to move slowly and speak calmly when dealing with a skunk, so Bat made sure to give Thor plenty of warning that he was about to be picked up.

This time, Bat could have sworn that when he slid his hand beneath Thor's soft little body, the kit sort of hopped, like he wanted to help Bat lift him.

Bat stood up straight, cradling Thor with both hands. He walked over to his beanbag chair and lowered himself gently down, being careful not to jostle the kit.

"Hi there, Thor," Bat said again. He leaned back in the beanbag and rested Thor on his chest, so the kit's little face was close to his.

Thor's black whiskers tickled Bat's cheek as the kit leaned in close. His nose was cool and dry, and sort of rough, like a cat's nose.

"Aww," said Bat, "you missed me." He stroked Thor's bright wide stripe, which started right between the kit's shiny black eyes and arched up over the top of his head, between his tiny black ears, trailing down his back, and stretching all the way to the tip of his tail.

Thor's fur was soft—not as soft as Babycakes's fur, but still pretty soft—until it came to his tail. Here, the fur was more like bristly hair, and when Thor got excited he could puff his tail out to make it look three times as big.

There was a gentle knock on Bat's door.

"Come in," he said.

It was Janie. She peered through the crack of the door as she slowly opened it, and then she came inside. "Hi, Bat," she said.

"Hi," Bat answered. "What do you want?"

"Nothing," said Janie. "I just thought I'd come visit you and Thor." She walked across the room and sat cross-legged on the floor near Bat. "How's he doing?"

"He's great," Bat said. "He's the best."

Janie reached out and scratched Thor behind his ears. Bat appreciated how slowly she moved and how gentle she was.

"Hey," Janie said after a moment, "I have an idea."

She got up and left, and Bat heard her going into her room next door. When she came back, she was holding a pink hairbrush, and she had her camera strung around her neck.

"Do you think Thor would like to be brushed?" she asked.

Bat shrugged. "Maybe."

Janie sat back down and handed the hairbrush to Bat, who sat up straighter, lowering Thor to his lap.

"Isn't this your brush?" he asked.

"Yes, but I have two," Janie said. "Thor can have this one."

"To keep?" Bat asked.

"To keep," Janie said.

Bat let Thor smell the brush first, and then he ran the bristles down Thor's back. The little skunk stiffened at first, surprised, but after a few strokes, he relaxed into Bat's lap, sort of flattening out, as Bat brushed him some more.

"Hey, he likes it!" Janie said. She snapped a picture.

"Yes," said Bat, smiling. "I guess that you and Thor have something in common after all."

Janie laughed. "You can brush my hair later, if you want," she said. "But only if you use a different brush."

CHAPTER 7
An Idea

///

By Wednesday, Bat had given a lot of thought to the Babycakes situation, as he had taken to calling it. *Of course* he would love to be Babycakes's caretaker over the summer. Who wouldn't?

But Bat was already Thor's caretaker, and he didn't think it would be fair to either of the animals for him to accept the position. What if Babycakes made Thor nervous, and Mom started to worry that he might spray or something, and then she decided that they should release Thor early?

Bat pictured Thor scampering away, his fluffy black-and-white tail disappearing into the bushes at the regional park, which Mom had already decided would make a good "forever home" for Thor.

What if that was the last thing Bat ever saw of Thor? That white stripe, the rear end of him, leaving Bat forever?

It was too much to imagine. Thinking about it, in the back seat of the car on the way to school, made the whole world seem too loud, too bright, too *much* to bear. Bat reached into his backpack and pulled out the earmuffs he sometimes liked to wear when things were feeling too intense.

They helped with the road sounds on the outside of Bat, but not with the swirling riot of feelings on the inside of Bat.

Thor was in his carrier on the seat right next to him, and Bat rubbed his fingers against the mesh. Thor scuffled over and pressed his cool dark nose against Bat's fingers.

There. That helped. Bat felt himself calming down.

Bat saw Mom glance up into her rearview mirror to check on him. He didn't feel like looking at her eyes. He looked at his lap instead.

"Are you okay, Bat?" Mom asked.

Bat rocked a little. "I'm going to tell Mr. Grayson that Jenny should be Babycakes's caretaker this summer," he said at last.

"Oh," said Mom.

"She's the best choice," Bat said, loudly now. "I can't be his caretaker because I'm already Thor's caretaker, and Israel can't be his caretaker because he's leaving for the first part of the summer to go visit his cousin, and Jenny visits Babycakes the third most, after me and Israel, so she's the best choice."

"I see," said Mom.

They had arrived at the school, but Mom didn't seem in a hurry for Bat to get out of the car. She pulled into a parking space, put the car in park, and turned off the engine. Then she turned around so that she was facing Bat.

"I was thinking," Mom said, "about what a great caretaker you have been for Thor. The best caretaker a skunk could have."

"I love him," Bat said. His fingers rubbed against the carrier's zipper.

"I know," Mom said. "And I was thinking . . . you have been such a great caretaker to Thor that it might be a good idea, after we release him in a month or so, to find you a pet of your own, at the animal shelter. Maybe a dog or a cat?"

"I've got to go," Bat said, and he pulled his fingers away from the carrier so quickly that Thor, who had been half asleep with his forehead pushed up against Bat's fingers, was startled awake.

Bat unclicked his seat belt and pushed open the car door. "See you later," he said, and he didn't wait to hear his mom's response. He closed the door and headed for the school, the weight of his backpack feeling like a million pounds.

Mom honked two short, friendly honks, like she always did, but Bat didn't look back. He didn't even wave good-bye.

CHAPTER 8
To Jenny, From Bat

"I think Jenny should take Babycakes home for the summer," Bat told Mr. Grayson, who was standing near the door to the classroom.

"That's not a bad idea," Mr. Grayson said, "if you're sure you don't want to do it?"

"It's not that I don't *want* to," Bat said. "It's that I *can't*."

"Okay," said Mr. Grayson. "It's settled, then. I'll

see if Jenny is interested in the job."

Satisfied, if not exactly happy, Bat went to his desk and sat down. He watched as other students came into the classroom, and when Jenny arrived, her brown hair puffing out from her head, her face smiling, like it almost always seemed to do, Bat watched as Mr. Grayson pulled her aside and asked her a question.

"*Do* I!" Jenny said loudly, her already-smiling face smiling even more widely. "Of course I do!"

"So, just check with your parents and let me know tomorrow, then, for sure," Mr. Grayson said.

"Oh, they'll say yes," Jenny said, sounding certain. "They always say yes to animals."

They sounded like good parents to Bat. Babycakes would be happy at Jenny's house for the summer. Bat settled more comfortably in his seat as Mr. Grayson started talking about math. He got out his pencil and his math book, ready to do some work.

But then a terrible thought occurred to Bat. If Jenny's parents always said yes to animals . . . how many animals might already be living at her house?

Bat got an awful feeling that maybe he'd made a huge mistake. His hand shot up into the air.

"Yes, Bat?" said Mr. Grayson. "Do you have a question?"

"Yes," said Bat. He turned to face Jenny, who sat two rows over from him. "How many animals do you have at your house? And what kind?"

A few kids started to laugh.

This wasn't funny, thought Bat. This was serious.

"Actually, Bat, I meant, do you have a question for *me*?" said Mr. Grayson. "About math?"

"No," said Bat. "I have a question for Jenny. Actually, I have several."

"I'm sorry, Bat," Mr. Grayson said. "You can ask Jenny your questions at recess. This is our last day of math work for the year, and I need to make sure we review a few more things." And then Mr. Grayson turned back to the board and started writing some equations.

Bat couldn't wait until recess. No way.

As quietly as he could, Bat tore a sheet of paper out of his notebook.

How many pets do you have? he wrote. *What kinds?*

He folded the paper in half, and then in half again, and then one more time, to make a neat little rectangle.

To Jenny, he wrote on the note.

He'd better put his name, too, Bat thought, so she'd know who the note was from.

From Bat, he added.

Israel sat in the seat next to Bat, between him and Jenny.

"Hey," Bat whispered, trying to get Israel's attention.

Israel looked over.

"Give this to Jenny," Bat whispered, his voice a little louder this time.

Israel looked at the note, and then at Bat, and then at Mr. Grayson, whose back was still turned to the class. "You're not supposed to pass notes in class," he said to Bat.

"I know that," Bat answered. "That's why I'm whispering."

Israel was a good friend. He shrugged, and then he took the note from Bat. He turned and tossed it onto Jenny's desk.

Just then, Mr. Grayson turned around. Bat saw Mr. Grayson see the note fly out of Israel's hand, arch across the aisle between the desks, and land in front of Jenny.

Israel was a good friend, and he shouldn't get in trouble for helping Bat.

Mr. Grayson was walking up the aisle toward Jenny's desk.

Bat said quickly, "Israel didn't send the note! I did! Israel shouldn't be in trouble."

Mr. Grayson stopped just next to Jenny's desk. She still hadn't touched the note. It sat there, a little white rectangle. Mr. Grayson flipped it over and read what Bat had written: *To Jenny, From Bat.* He smiled.

"Bat, no one is in trouble. I can see it's very

important to you to speak with Jenny."

"Yes," Bat said, relieved. "It is."

Mr. Grayson handed the note to Jenny. "I believe this is for you," he said, "but please put it away until recess. Okay?"

"Okay," said Jenny, and she stuck the note in the side pocket of her backpack.

Mr. Grayson went back to the front of the classroom. He picked up the marker again, and he went back to talking about math.

Bat felt all sorts of things mixed up together:

1. He felt relieved that no one was in trouble.

2. He felt worried over what kinds of pets Jenny might have.

3. He felt itchy and uncomfortable, knowing he had to wait for an hour and a half to get any answers to his questions.

Bat hated waiting.

CHAPTER 9
Under the Play Structure

If Bat had been a mayfly, *maybe* the wait from math time to recess would have seemed even longer, but Bat found that hard to believe.

As it was, Bat stared at the hands of the classroom clock, over the whiteboard at the front of the room, absolutely certain that it had to be broken. There was *no way* that seconds were supposed to last that long!

Every bone in his body felt as if it were vibrating with tension; every muscle ached with being squeezed so tight. Bat's fingers, wrapped around the edge of his seat, practically froze into claws, he gripped so fiercely.

A couple of times, Israel leaned over and said, "Dude! Relax."

But Bat could not relax.

At last, it was time for recess. Bat stood up and headed straight for Jenny's desk, but she was rushed out of the classroom by Lucca and Mei before Bat could get to her.

And then there was sort of a traffic jam at the classroom door, where Ramon and Henry were goofing around and Ramon accidentally knocked Henry's open bag of trail mix to the floor. Everybody dropped down to their knees to help pick up all the loose almonds and chocolate chips and raisins, even Mr. Grayson, and even though Bat said "Excuse me" very loud and forcefully, no one got out of his way.

"Just a *second*, Bat," said Ramon, sounding kind of loud and irritated, but of course it *wasn't* just a second, it was more like at least sixty seconds before they all stood up again and filtered out of the classroom and Bat could at last get through.

Outside, the playground was really hot and bright in a way that Bat didn't like. He felt the rays of the sun glaring down at him as if they were being directed through a magnifying glass. He put a hand up over his eyes and squinted as he scanned the yard, looking for Jenny.

Finally, he saw her, with Mei and Lucca, sitting in the shade underneath the climbing structure.

"What kinds of pets do you have?" Bat asked, getting down on his hands and knees to scoot next to the girls beneath the jungle gym.

"I've got two cats," Mei said brightly.

"Not you," Bat said, waving a hand in Mei's direction. "Jenny."

"I've got a golden retriever, a cat, two parakeets, and a tortoise," Jenny said. She was peeling an orange.

"Is your dog gentle?" Bat asked.

"Uh-huh," Jenny said. She made a neat little pile of orange peels and tore off a segment of the orange, popping it in her mouth.

Bat felt a little better hearing that Jenny's golden retriever was gentle. Probably that meant Babycakes would be fine at her house.

"We used to have three tortoises—a big one and two babies—but we had to give the babies away because my cat kept flipping them over onto their backs! She can't do that to the big tortoise, though, so we got to keep that one."

"Tortoises can die if they're flipped on their

backs!" Bat said. "They can't flip themselves right side up again!"

"I know," said Jenny, eating another slice of her orange and then offering one to Bat. "That's why we gave them away."

Bat ignored the orange slice. "But your cat might try to hurt Babycakes, too. I don't think you're the best person to be her caretaker over the summer. Unless you can find a different home for your cat."

"No offense, Bat," said Jenny, "but it isn't up to you. Mr. Grayson said I could take Babycakes home. And anyway, she'll be in a cage in my room. The cat won't even be anywhere near her."

This wasn't good enough for Bat. Without another word, he scooted himself out from under the climbing structure and headed back toward the school building. Mr. Grayson was just going to have to sort this out.

CHAPTER 10
The Last Day of Third Grade

///

But Mr. Grayson *didn't* sort it out.

"I'm sorry, Bat," he said when Bat came in from recess, "but I've already offered Babycakes to Jenny. I'm sure her parents will say no if it isn't a good fit."

Bat spent most of that day and the next hoping that Jenny's parents would have more sense than Jenny.

But on Friday morning, Jenny announced, "My mom's going to pick me up this afternoon, and she's bringing the big car so there will be room in the back for Babycakes and her stuff!"

Bat's eyes filled with hot tears. Israel leaned over and said something, but Bat did not want to talk to Israel.

And because it was the last day of the school year, nothing happened in its usual order. There was no math time, or reading time, or any of that. There were games, and a pizza party at lunch, and then all the kids signed each other's yearbooks, which was really just a notebook Mr. Grayson had made for them with pictures of the things the class had done that year.

Bat spent yearbook-signing time sitting with Babycakes. The bunny chewed contentedly and unremarkably on her hay, completely oblivious of the giant change that was about to occur.

Mr. Grayson came over to Bat and Babycakes. "You seem worried, my friend," he said to Bat.

"I am worried," Bat said.

Mr. Grayson sighed. "Bat," he said, "do you know how old Babycakes is?"

Bat hadn't ever really thought about it. Babycakes was full-grown, Bat knew that much, and angora rabbits live between seven and twelve years, so she must be somewhere between two (since she was already full-grown when Bat had met her last September) and twelve (since she was still alive) . . . but other than that, he didn't really know.

"Three?" Bat guessed.

"Wow," said Mr. Grayson. "That's pretty good! Yep, she's about three and a half years old. I got Babycakes as a young bunny when I first got this job at the Saw Whet School, and this is my third year here."

"You've taught third grade for three years and you have a three-year-old class pet," Bat said.

Mr. Grayson laughed. "I guess so. Anyway, Bat, do you know what that means?"

Bat didn't.

"It means that this will be the third summer that Babycakes will be going home with a student. And come September, it'll be Babycakes's fourth fall at Saw Whet School, and in my classroom."

Next year, Bat would be in the fourth grade. Mr. Grayson wouldn't be his teacher anymore. Bat hadn't really thought about that.

He looked over at Mr. Grayson. He saw his orange high-top tennis shoes and the funny way Mr. Grayson folded his jeans at the bottoms— pegged, he called them. He saw that Mr. Grayson was wearing two silver rings on his left hand and a brass ring on his right hand. He saw that Mr. Grayson must be trying again to grow a mustache, something he'd done twice before that year, with not very much success.

And Bat realized how much he was going to miss his teacher. Maybe even as much as he would miss Babycakes.

"I think I'd like to be in third grade again next year," Bat said.

Mr. Grayson smiled. "I'm going to miss you too, Bat," he said. "But you'll be in the room right next door, with Ms. Imani, and you can come and visit me and Babycakes as much as you want."

"What if I want to visit you and Babycakes every day?"

"Then you can come every day," Mr. Grayson said.

Babycakes had finished eating her hay. She hopped around, her cute little nose twitching, like she was looking for something.

"I'm worried that Jenny's cat will hurt Baby-cakes," Bat said, "or maybe scare her."

"I know," Mr. Grayson said. "I'll tell you what I'll do. I'm going to give Jenny's mom your mom's phone number, okay? And I'll tell her that if there is any sign that it isn't going to work out at their house, they should call you and let you know. And then you can help figure out a backup plan. Okay?"

It wasn't per-fect. But it was better than nothing.

"Okay," Bat said.

Mr. Grayson reached out his hand, and Bat took it. Mr. Grayson pulled him up to standing. "Now, come on," he said. "Let's go get some signatures in that yearbook of yours."

It was an Every-Other Friday, which meant that when the last day of school was officially over, Dad was waiting for Bat in the parking lot.

"Hi, sport!" he said, leaning over to unlock the passenger door.

"Hi," Bat said, pushing forward the front seat and sliding behind it into the narrow back seat. He didn't like it when Dad called him "sport," but today he had bigger things to worry about.

Dad looked at him. "You don't seem very happy for a kid on the last day of school," he said.

"That's because I wish it wasn't the last day of school," Bat said.

Dad laughed. "I don't think in all my years of school, college years included, I ever said those words." He turned back around and steered the car toward the school's exit. They drove past Jenny's mom's car, where Mr. Grayson was helping load Babycakes's stuff into the trunk. Jenny was standing nearby, holding Babycakes in her travel case.

As they drove past, Bat's dad waved at Mr. Grayson, who waved back.

"Have a great summer, Bat!" Mr. Grayson called.

And then they were out of the parking lot and down the road, and that was the end of third grade.

CHAPTER 11
Pizza Night

//

Maybe Bat wasn't happy about the school year being over, but Janie was.

Bat and Dad picked her up from outside her school, where she stood surrounded by a big circle of friends. They were all laughing and hugging, and then Janie took a bunch of pictures of everyone with her camera, and Bat had to wait an extra five minutes for Janie to finish saying good-bye.

By the time Janie finally slid into the front seat, slinging her full backpack into the rear seat with Bat, he was almost twitchy with anger.

"You shouldn't make us wait like that!" Bat's words came out loudly, and it felt good, like finally letting go of a sneeze held in too long.

"Jeez, Bat, you don't need to yell at me," Janie said. She buckled her seat belt. "It's the last day of school! I was just saying good-bye to my friends."

"It's not like you won't get to see them anymore,"

Bat said. "It's not like they're going to Canada." Then Bat realized that he hadn't said good-bye to Israel, who *was* going to Canada, and Bat wouldn't see him for weeks.

"Okay, all right," Dad said. He turned on his blinker, looked over his shoulder, and then pulled into traffic. "Everybody calm down."

Bat didn't *want* to calm down. His body felt hot and itchy and uncomfortable, and the seat belt pressed on his collarbone like it was trying to choke him.

Dad's window was rolled partway down, and the sound of the wind coming into the car was so, so loud. Bat put his hands over his ears and rocked forward and back.

"So," Dad said—loudly—"we're going to go out to dinner tonight to celebrate the end of the school year!"

"Great!" said Janie. "Can we get pizza?"

"Actually," said Dad, "we're going to go some-where a little fancier. And a friend of mine is going to meet us there."

"A friend?" said Janie. "What friend?"

"Please roll up your window," Bat said. But Dad didn't. Maybe he didn't hear Bat.

"A new friend," Dad said. "You haven't met her before."

"*Her?*" asked Janie.

"Roll up your window!" yelled Bat.

Dad rolled up his window. "All right, sport, you don't have to yell," he said to Bat. Then he turned to Janie and said, "Yes. My friend is a 'her.'"

But they didn't go out to pizza. Or anywhere.

"I have a terrible headache," Janie said, almost as soon as they got home to Dad's apartment. "I'm going to go take a nap."

And she went into the bedroom and closed the door.

Later, when it was time to get ready to leave for dinner, Janie said, "I still don't feel good."

"You'll be fine," Dad said. He was wearing a new shirt, blue-and-brown plaid, and he'd even taken off his usual baseball cap. His hair, Bat thought, looked kind of stiff.

"I'm not going," Janie said.

"But we're going to a restaurant," Bat said. "You love restaurants."

"You'll have to go without me," Janie said. And she went back into her room and closed the door—loudly.

Dad tried to convince Janie to get up and get ready. He asked nicely. He tried to make a deal. He even yelled a little. But nothing Dad said could convince Janie to get out of bed. She just lay there with her pillow over her head, saying nothing.

Bat watched from the little kitchen, feeling unsettled. He couldn't remember Janie ever complaining of a headache bad enough to stop her from going out to eat.

"Do we need to call a doctor?" Bat asked.

"No," Dad said.

Finally, Dad gave up. He sighed and pinched the top of his nose, like maybe *he* had a headache now too.

Then he went back into the living room, sat on the couch, and made two phone calls. The first was to his new friend.

"Hi," he said. "It's me. I'm sorry, but tonight isn't going to work after all. Janie doesn't . . . feel very well. Okay, we'll do it another time." After he hung up, he grabbed his baseball cap from the coffee table and pulled it back on. Now he looked more like Dad.

Then he made his second call. "Hello," he said. "Delivery, please. I'd like a large pizza—half cheese, half pepperoni."

"And breadsticks!" said Bat. Breadsticks were Janie's favorite.

"And breadsticks," Dad said into the phone.

CHAPTER 12

Doughnuts for Breakfast

//

In the morning, Janie's headache was all gone, and she felt good enough to ride bikes into town for doughnuts.

Bat loved riding bikes. He loved the special bike paths, the way they had a broken yellow line painted right down the center, so that bikes going one way were on one side of the path, and bikes going the other way were on the other side of the path, just like they were cars driving on the road.

He loved how the crosswalks made a friendly chirping sound to let you know when it was your turn to go across the street. He loved going across the little bridge, and he loved parking his bike in the rack downtown, stringing the chain between the spokes of the wheel and clicking the lock into place.

Janie and Dad loved riding bikes too. It was something all three of them liked to do together. The whole world seemed to be in a good mood—the birds, chirping in the trees; the other bicyclists, who smiled and dinged their bells to say hello; the motorists, who were polite at crosswalks, leaving plenty of room so that Bat felt safe while he crossed; the dogs with waggy tails, on one end of their leashes, and the people walking them, on the other end.

There was a big bright-blue sky and no clouds at all, not even the wispy ones. Maybe, Bat thought as he chained up his bike and spun the numbers on the lock, summer would be okay, after all.

Dad smiled as he held open the door to the doughnut shop, the doorbell tinkling as they entered. Bat followed Janie inside, thinking about which kind of doughnut he would choose today. Maybe a tiger's tail, because he liked the name so much. Or a bear claw. He headed straight for the glass case to look at all his choices.

"Suzette," Dad said, "you're here already!"

Bat looked away from the doughnuts and to a lady sitting at one of the tables, holding a cup of coffee. She stood up when she saw them, and she smiled a wide friendly smile at them.

"You must be Janie and Bat," she said, holding out her hand. "I'm Suzette. It's so nice to meet you."

Janie just stood there, even though she was usually the first person to say hello and do the polite things like hand shaking. Bat looked back and forth between Janie and the lady's outstretched hand, waiting to see what would happen.

"Janie, Bat," Dad said, "this is my friend Suzette. Say hello."

"Hello," said Bat. And then, because Suzette was still holding out her hand, Bat shook it.

"Your fingers are warm," he said.

Suzette smiled. "That's because I was just holding my cup of coffee," she said.

"You didn't tell me your *friend* was going to be here," Janie said to Dad.

"Janie, don't be rude," Dad said in a rude voice.

Janie crossed her arms. "I don't think I want any doughnuts after all," she said. "I'm going to wait outside by the bikes." And then she turned and left, shoving hard on the door so that the little friendly bell clanged loudly.

Bat didn't know what to do. He'd never seen Janie be rude to a grown-up before. Maybe her head was hurting again.

"I'm so sorry about that," Dad was saying to Suzette. "I don't know what's gotten into her. She's usually so polite."

"Didn't you tell them I was going to be here?" Suzette asked.

That was something Bat *did* know. "No," he told her. "He didn't."

"Oh, Calvin," Suzette said, and she shook her head.

"Can I still have a doughnut?" Bat asked.

Dad ignored him. "I should have told them you were meeting us here," he said to Suzette. "I thought it might be easier this way."

"Easier for *you*," Suzette said. "Not easier for Janie."

"Maybe her headache is back," Bat said.

Suzette rubbed her forehead like maybe *she* had a headache too, and then Bat started to worry that something was going around, and that maybe he could catch it as well. "I think I'll wait outside with Janie," he said. "Dad, will you please get me a bear claw?"

"Sure, sport," Dad said.

Bat turned toward the door. Behind him, he heard Suzette say, "For such a smart guy, Calvin, sometimes you do pretty unsmart things."

Hearing Suzette calling Dad by his first name gave Bat an uncomfortable feeling in his stomach. Maybe he was getting sick too.

CHAPTER 13
Planning for the Future

///

"Remember," Mom said, looking at Bat in her rearview mirror, "Laurence is the boss, okay? You do what he says." They were on their way to Mom's vet clinic. The first week of summer, Bat and Janie had spent the mornings at home together while Mom worked, but this week Janie was taking a class at the pool, and Bat got to go to the clinic with Mom.

"What if he tells me to let all the dogs out of their pens?" Bat asked.

"Laurence would never do that. You know he wouldn't."

"I know," Bat said. "But what if he does?"

Mom smiled. "Do whatever Laurence says, *within reason*. Okay?"

"Okay," Bat answered.

Mom turned on her blinker, waited for a break in traffic, and turned left into the parking lot.

There was the small redbrick building with the neat sign that read "Valerie Tam, DVM."

Doctor of veterinary medicine. That was what Bat was going to be too, one day.

But today he would be assistant to veterinary technician Laurence, which was also a pretty good thing to be.

Mom parked the car in her usual spot and

turned off the engine. Bat, whose hand had been resting on top of Thor's carrying case, unlatched his seat belt, opened his door, and scooted out of the car, bringing Thor with him.

"He's getting heavy," Bat told Mom as they headed for the clinic's front door.

"He's getting big," Mom agreed, but Bat was glad that was all she said. He was in a particularly good mood, and he didn't need any reminders that Thor was almost old enough to be released.

The low brick building had a heavy glass door, which Mom opened. Bat angled through it, being careful not to bang Thor's carrying case on the way in.

It was difficult for Bat to put into words the feelings he had about the veterinary clinic. It was a lot of wonderful feelings, mixed together like soup ingredients.

He could feel his face stretching into a grin as he looked around the clinic waiting room. It smelled like lavender and peppermint because of the cleaning spray they used to clean up pet accidents. Then the phone rang, and Suzanne answered it from her spot behind the counter. "Dr. Tam's office," she said cheerily.

And that made Bat feel proud. Because Dr. Tam was his mom, and this was her clinic.

From somewhere in the back, Bat heard a dog bark. And that made him feel excited, because it reminded him that this building was full of animals, and there was nothing that Bat loved more than animals.

Suzanne finished her phone call and said, "Good morning, Dr. Tam. Good morning, Bat. Good morning, Thor."

Bat lifted Thor's carrying case and set it on the

counter so that Suzanne could get a good look at the skunk kit, who was awake and rustling around. She rubbed her fingers against the mesh door to scratch Thor's face; he pressed his leathery dark nose flat against it and sniffed her hand.

"My, what a handsome skunk you are," Suzanne said admiringly. That was something Bat really loved about coming to the vet clinic; everyone here loved animals—almost as much as Bat did.

"My dad's new friend's name is Suzette," Bat told Suzanne.

"Oh?" said Suzanne. "That's almost the same as my name."

"Almost," Bat said.

"Your dad has a new friend, Bat?" his mom asked.

He nodded. "We met her at the doughnut shop, but only for a minute, because Janie felt sick. We took our doughnuts back to Dad's apartment and ate them there instead."

"Janie didn't tell me she felt sick when you guys were with your dad," Mom said.

"She felt a lot better when we got back to the apartment," Bat said. "She ate two doughnuts."

Bat looked up at Suzanne and saw that she was looking at his mom with her eyebrows raised in two arches. "Don't worry," he said, "I don't think it was contagious. I feel fine."

Suzanne looked at him and smiled. "Thank you, Bat. I'm not worried about getting sick."

Mom cleared her throat. "Okay," she said, "let's head back to the kennels. Suzanne, do I have any messages?"

Suzanne handed Bat's mom a small stack of thin rectangular yellow sheets.

"Thank you," Mom said, and she pulled open the door that led into the back.

Bat picked up Thor's carrier and followed her through the door, watching as she took her white coat from its hook, just like she always did, and put it on. He read the words embroidered on it: "Dr. Tam, DVM." And he let  himself imagine that he was the one putting on the coat for a day of seeing patients.

"When I grow up and become a vet," Bat said, "maybe we could both work here. And we could put a second hook on the wall, and we could hang our coats next to each other's, and it wouldn't matter who wore which coat, because we would both be Dr. Tam, DVM."

Mom's fingers were buttoning her coat, but they stopped when Bat spoke. She reached over and put a hand gently on top of his head, a warm soft weight that Bat liked. "There is nothing that would make me happier," she said.

Bat had his mom's warm hand on his head, and Thor's carrier in his hand, and a whole day of helping at the vet clinic in front of him. He took in a deep breath of lavender-peppermint, and he felt wonderful.

CHAPTER 14
An Assistant's Assistant

In the back room, in front of the row of kennels, Laurence stood looking over a list on a clipboard. He had a pencil in his hand.

"Hi, Laurence," Bat said. "We're here!"

Laurence looked up and smiled. "Bat Boy! I've been looking forward to seeing you and Thor. I haven't gotten to babysit him since summer started."

"It's been nice staying home," Bat said. "I've had lots of time to work with Thor. I'm trying to clicker train him."

"Are you?" Laurence said. "How's it going?"

"Pretty good. I can get him to wait for a treat for ten seconds or so."

"Hmm," Laurence said. "Are you sure it's a good idea to spend time training him? After all, pretty soon he's going to be out on his own."

Bat changed the subject. "What are we going to do today?"

Laurence looked at his list. "Let's see . . . Mrs. Herrera will be dropping off Pumpkin this morning for a bath and a nail trim. Want to help me with that?"

"Yes," said Bat. "It will take at least two people to give Pumpkin a bath. He's enormous!"

"He's too big for the washbasin," Laurence

agreed. "We'll have to use the big tub."

"I think he's pure mastiff," Bat said happily. He took Thor's carrier over to the far kennel, where Laurence had already laid out fresh towels for him. He set the carrier on the ground and unzipped its door. Thor peeked out his head, snuffed around a bit, and then waddled slowly out of the carrier, straight toward Bat.

Bat picked him up, one hand under each of Thor's armpits, and brought the skunk up to his face. "Hello, little buddy," he whispered, and then he kissed the very beginning of Thor's white stripe, just above his leathery dark nose. Thor nudged Bat's face with his nose and tucked his head into the crook of Bat's neck, so Bat hugged him close and rocked a little, the way that Thor liked.

"Wow," said Laurence. "Thor really does like you!"

"I like him, too," Bat answered.

"Well," said Laurence, "we all like Thor, but he never snuggles with me like that when I'm taking care of him."

Bat didn't say anything to this, but he felt pleased to hear that Thor snuggled with him more than Laurence. Smiling, Bat turned to the kennel and tipped Thor toward it. Obligingly, the skunk kit waddled inside and began to snuff around in the blankets.

Bat shut the kennel door, double-checking to make sure it was latched.

And just in time, too—Suzanne's voice came over the intercom, sounding a little panicked. "Laurence," she said, "Pumpkin is here! Please come get him . . . right away!"

"What do you say, Bat Boy? Want to fetch Pumpkin with me?"

Bat did.

In the waiting room, Mrs. Herrera held tightly to Pumpkin's thick leather leash. On the other end, Pumpkin strained forward, toward the counter, where he must have smelled the treat dish. Slowly, Mrs. Herrera was towed forward, her feet sliding across the linoleum.

"Oh, good," said Suzanne when Bat and Laurence came through the door. "That was fast."

Laurence unwound the leash from around Mrs. Herrera's hand. She sighed with relief, and Bat noticed that her hand was blotchy red and white from where the leash had pinched it.

"Pumpkin," said Laurence, his voice gentle but stern, "sit."

Pumpkin's dark-tipped ears perked up, and he flopped his muscular haunches down, looking up at Laurence. A thick, clear ribbon of drool stretched toward the ground.

"He's always so good for you," Mrs. Herrera said.

"I can't believe it," Bat said, "but I think Pumpkin is even bigger than he was when Janie and I came over!"

"No," said Mrs. Herrera quickly. "He hasn't grown any more."

"We'll weigh him today when we give him his bath," Laurence said.

"No need for that," Mrs. Herrera said.

"Well, we keep a record," Laurence said.

She sighed. "Weigh him if you have to, I guess, but he isn't an ounce heavier, I can tell you that."

"He's not an *ounce* heavier," Bat said, "because he's *pounds* heavier!"

Laurence and Suzanne both laughed, but Mrs. Herrera sighed again. "I'll be back to pick him up this afternoon."

She left through the glass door, and Bat took one of the treats from the dish on the counter and held it out to Pumpkin, whose long pink tongue scooped it out of Bat's hand in one lick.

"What do you say, Bat?" Laurence said. "Are you ready to get to work?"

Bat was. But just then, the glass door slammed open, and a voice said, "Something is wrong with Babycakes!"

CHAPTER 15
Head Tilt and Snuffles

It was Jenny. She'd burst through the door, her hair wild, her face wet with tears. She seemed surprised to see Bat standing there, but she repeated, "Something's wrong with Babycakes."

"Is Babycakes your pet, dear?" Suzanne said from behind the counter.

"Babycakes is our class pet," Bat said. His head began to buzz as if it were filled with angry bees, and his stomach twisted. "Suzanne, go get Mom."

Suzanne stood up from her desk and disappeared into the back. Laurence left too, to take Pumpkin to the kennels.

An older lady pushed through the door. She held Babycakes, wrapped in a towel. Bat could see thick streams of mucus coming from the rabbit's nostrils and noticed that Babycakes's head was sort of flopped over to one side.

"Is the vet available?" said the lady—maybe she was Jenny's grandmother.

"Okay, I'm back," said Laurence. "What seems to be the problem?" Bat felt a grateful wave of relief that Laurence had come back so quickly.

"It's Babycakes," Bat said. Jenny was crying loudly now. She'd dropped down onto the vinyl bench and had her head in her hands.

Laurence stretched out his hands. "May I?" he asked.

The lady who was probably Jenny's grandmother

handed him the bundled-up bunny. "She's had a cold for a couple of days, but we thought it was just a case of the sniffles. And then this morning she was holding her head funny—tilted to the side like that."

Laurence took Babycakes and held her gently.

"Hey there, little lady," he cooed.

Bat came up close and peered at the bunny. He could only see her head, since the rest of her was swaddled tightly, but he noticed that Babycakes's eyes looked kind of dull and watery. A bubble of mucus grew out of her left nostril.

"I shouldn't have let you be Babycakes's care-taker," Bat said.

Jenny cried louder.

"Let's focus on the patient, Bat Boy," said Laurence.

Laurence was right.

"Here I am," said Bat's mom, emerging from the back, followed by Suzanne. "Hello, Babycakes. Feeling a little under the weather, are you?"

"She's congested and her eyes are watery and she's tilting her head to the left," Bat said.

"Okay," said Mom. "Let's take her to the exam room."

Laurence led the way. Bat followed. His mom had dropped her arm around Jenny's shoulders, and Jenny sniffled and hiccupped and wiped her eyes. The lady who was probably Jenny's grandmother brought up the end of the line.

It was a very crowded exam room.

Laurence set Babycakes down on the metal exam table and unwound the towel she was wrapped in. He kept a hand on Babycakes's back to keep her from hopping away, even though Babycakes didn't look like she wanted to hop anywhere.

Mom had taken her stethoscope out of her pocket and placed the ear tips in her ears. She pressed the other end, called the bell, to Babycakes's side. She would listen to the bunny's heart and lungs, Bat knew.

He couldn't help with the listening, but he could pay close attention to Babycakes's condition. He noticed that Babycakes's fluffy coat was

smooth and well brushed, without any matting or tangles. That meant that Jenny had been grooming her every day.

And it was hard to tell without holding the bunny, but it didn't look like Babycakes had lost much weight, if any.

And her paws were clean, which meant that Jenny had been keeping her enclosure nice and fresh.

Bat's mom took the stethoscope off and placed it back into her pocket. "Her lungs sound clear and her heart is strong," she reported.

"Jenny's parents are out of town, and I've been taking care of her and her brothers for the last few days," said Jenny's grandmother. "We didn't notice anything wrong with the bunny until the day before yesterday, when she started to look like she had a little cold, and then this morning when we went to feed her, she was doing this funny thing with her head, so we brought her right in."

Jenny kept crying.

"Rabbits don't get colds," Bat said.

Bat's mom shone a light into Babycakes's eyes. Her head was still tilted, and when the light hit her left eye, the one on the low side of her head, she didn't blink.

"They don't get people's colds, but they do get respiratory infections that can look like a cold," Bat's mom said. "It's called the snuffles." Laurence still stood with his hands gently holding Babycakes. The bunny was so fluffy that his fingers disappeared into her fur.

Bat's mom lifted Babycakes's right ear and shone the light inside. "Ah," she said. "It looks like the snuffles has caused an ear infection. That's what's causing the head tilt. Bat, Jenny, do you want to take a look?"

Bat did. He walked over to the exam table and peered into Babycakes's ear. It was red and swollen looking.

"Is she going to be okay?" cried Jenny.

Bat's mom turned off the light and stroked Babycakes's tilted head. "I think she'll be fine," she said. "We'll keep her here for a few days to monitor her and start her on a course of antibiotics. She'll need eye drops for her left eye too; she won't be able to blink that eye until the head tilt resolves."

"Bat was right," Jenny said quietly. "I shouldn't have been the one to take Babycakes home. It's my fault she's sick."

Bat looked again at Babycakes's smooth, tangle-free coat. Her clean, unstained feet. Her nice plump body.

"You are a good caretaker," he said. "You've taken good care of Babycakes."

Jenny wiped her eyes. They were red and swollen, and her nose was dripping.

"Babycakes's coat is brushed, and her feet are clean, and she's been well fed," he continued. "It's not your fault she's sick."

Jenny took a deep, ragged breath, and then she smiled. "Thank you, Bat," she said. "That's nice of you to say."

"I said it because it's true," Bat answered.

CHAPTER 16
House Call

//

It turned out that Babycakes had to spend four nights at the vet clinic. Mr. Grayson came that very first day, as soon as Jenny's grandmother told him what had happened. He'd come to the clinic straight from soccer practice, and Bat thought he looked sort of funny in knee-high socks and shorts. He even had a sweatband on.

Bat's mom had told him not to worry about payment; Babycakes was a "pro bono case," she said, which Bat knew meant that his mom was taking care of the bunny for free, the way she had for the hawk who had been shot with a BB gun and had a broken wing.

And Bat went with his mom to the clinic every day for the whole week. He had a nice routine: after settling Thor into a kennel, he put drops in Babycakes's eye and spent some time combing her coat and giving her gentle pats. Then he'd help Laurence with whatever Laurence needed: mostly baths and nail trims and walks for dogs who were boarding overnight while their people were out of town. He and Laurence would eat lunch together at a nearby park, and twice Mom joined them, on slow days. After lunch, Bat would take Thor out of his kennel into an unoccupied exam room to give him some food and let him snuff around. Then Thor would curl up in Bat's lap while Bat read a book from the library.

It was pretty perfect. Bat couldn't think of a better way to spend his summer.

On Friday, Babycakes was well enough to go home to Jenny's house. The bunny was holding her head almost straight again, and she could blink both of her eyes.

Jenny and her grandmother came to pick her up with a carrier that had a fresh, soft towel in the bottom of it. Jenny held open the door while Bat gently guided Babycakes inside. When the carrier was safely locked, Bat said, "She doesn't need the eye drops anymore, but you still have to give her antibiotics twice a day for another ten days. And if she starts to look worse or tilt her head or get mucusy, you need to bring her back right away."

"Okay, Bat, I know," said Jenny. "Your mom already told me and Grandma all that."

"Okay," said Bat. "I just wanted to make sure."

Jenny picked up the carrier by its handle. Her

grandmother was standing by the glass door that led outside. "You can come visit if you want, Bat," Jenny said. "If you want to check on Babycakes."

"When?" asked Bat.

Bat went to Jenny's house on Sunday. It was supposed to be an Every-Other Weekend, but Dad was out of town for work, so Mom drove him. She brought her little doctor's bag with her. "Might as well take a look at Babycakes, since we're driving there anyway," she said, and Bat felt his heart bursting with pride that his mom was doing a special vet visit just for Babycakes.

It turned out that Jenny didn't live very far away. Bat brought two carrots that he'd harvested from Thor's Garden as a get-well-soon present for Babycakes. He left the tops on because rabbits like the greens as much as they like the carrots, and also because there are different vitamins in the greens.

It was true that Jenny's house had lots of animals—and lots of people—but it was also true that her house had a nice, friendly feeling, and that it didn't *smell* like lots of animals and people lived there.

Babycakes was in a big, deep bathtub in Jenny's parents' bathroom. It was a hot day, and the bathtub was the coolest place in the whole house. "She can't jump out," Jenny said. "The sides are too high and slippery. And we can close the door to the bathroom so that the dog can't get in. Not that she wants to. She's a scaredy-cat."

Bat thought it was funny to call a dog a scaredy-cat.

"Our *actual* cat ignores Babycakes entirely," Jenny said.

Jenny had put Babycakes's plastic hutch inside the bathtub, and she was asleep inside it. Bat wasn't sure if they should wake her up, but Mom said it would be okay, and she lifted up the hutch and set it on the bathroom floor. Then she scooped Babycakes into her lap. She listened to her heart and lungs and looked in her eyes and ears and nose.

And even though Bat wasn't a vet, he could see that Babycakes was much better. Her little nose quivered and twitched with interest at everything Bat's mom did, and she kicked her back legs and tried to escape when Mom shone the light into her eyes.

Bat's mom laughed and set Babycakes back into the bathtub. "Okay, okay," she said. "I'm all done. She's looking good, Jenny! You're taking good care of her."

Jenny grinned.

Bat's mom went to have a cup of iced tea in the kitchen with Jenny's grandmother, who was still taking care of Jenny and her brothers, and Bat and Jenny sat on the edge of the tub and broke the carrots into little pieces, taking turns feeding them to Babycakes.

"That was scary," Jenny said after a few minutes. "I'm so glad Babycakes is going to be all right."

"Me too," said Bat, enjoying the soft tickling feeling of Babycakes's whiskers against his palm.

Babycakes finished the last bite of carrot and hopped around the bathtub, sniffing each corner as if she was hoping to find something more to eat.

Then Jenny said, "So, how much longer do you get to keep that skunk, before you have to let him go?"

The question ruined the good mood Bat had been in, watching Babycakes and enjoying how healthy she seemed. "I don't want to talk about Thor," he said.

"You *always* want to talk about Thor," Jenny answered.

Bat didn't say anything for a minute, but Jenny just waited. Finally, Bat said quietly, "I don't want to talk about Thor going away."

"Oh," said Jenny. "I understand."

The truth was that Bat's mom had brought up this topic the night before, and Bat hadn't wanted to talk about it then, either.

"He's nice and plump, and nights are warm now," Mom had said. "Really, I think Thor is big enough to take care of himself anytime. Maybe we can give him another week or two just to make sure."

Bat hadn't said anything to this. He had been sitting in a kitchen chair eating graham crackers, but when Mom had brought up the subject of Thor's release, he lost his appetite, and his mouth even felt too dry to swallow the bite in his mouth that he'd already chewed up.

He had wrapped his arms around himself and rocked a little, back and forth, and when his mom finished talking, he went to the bathroom and spit out the last bite of graham cracker and didn't come out for a long time.

Now the same question had followed him into Jenny's bathroom. Here, Bat didn't have a mouthful of graham cracker, but he had that same feeling, of wanting to spit something out, of the discomfort that came with the thought of Thor being gone from his life.

"Are you scared he won't be able to take care of himself?" Jenny asked.

Bat nodded, his throat too full to speak.

"If I had to let my dog or my cat go, I'd miss them so much," Jenny said.

Bat nodded again. Even though he couldn't make himself say the words, and even though it made him so sad to hear Jenny saying them, there was a relief to it, too, of hearing her talk about Bat's worst fears.

Bat and Jenny sat together on the edge of the cool, white bathtub.

Babycakes hopped over, her little nose twitching hopefully.

"We don't have any more carrots," Jenny told the bunny.

But Babycakes stayed there anyway, close by, like she was glad for their company, even if they didn't have anything else to give her.

CHAPTER 17
At the Pool

Janie had been spending most of her days at the city pool. It had a low diving board and a high diving board. It had long, neat rows of lounge chairs. It had a snack bar that sold pizza and pretzels and bottled water. It had a boys' locker room that had a drain in the middle of the floor. Janie said the girls' locker room also had a drain in the middle of its floor.

There was a little-kid pool that was shallow

all the way across. In the big pool, three lap-swimming lanes were sectioned off with plastic floating ropes that you weren't supposed to hang on. Those lanes were almost always taken by grown-ups, some of them very old, swimming seriously back and forth.

Janie loved the city pool. Bat did not.

It was crowded, and loud, and too bright. The concrete was rough and hot beneath Bat's feet. The air was sharp with the smell of chlorine. And no animals were allowed.

"It's not so bad, is it, sport?" Dad asked. It was an Every-Other Weekend, and Dad had let Janie choose the Saturday activity.

"Yes," said Bat. "It is."

He was wearing sunglasses, which helped, and he and his dad both wore baseball caps, which helped too. Bat had a long-sleeved swim shirt on because he hated the feeling of sunscreen on his body.

Dad found a couple of lounge chairs in the shade and spread out their towels. He lay back on one of them, closed his eyes, and said, "This is the life."

Bat tilted his lounge chair upright and sat. He felt hot and itchy inside the swim shirt.

Janie emerged from the girls' locker room and looked around. Bat waved until she saw him and watched as she walked across the concrete toward them.

"Wow, it's hot," she said when she arrived at their spot. "Bat, do you want to go jump in the water with me?"

"Not yet," Bat answered.

"Okay," said Janie. Then she said, "Dad, you're not expecting anyone else to meet us here, are you?"

Dad laughed. "No, Janie," he said. "Not today." He opened his eyes.

"Who would he be expecting?" Bat asked Janie.

"His girlfriend," Janie said, and her voice sounded funny.

"Dad has a girlfriend?"

"Yes, Bat," said Janie, sounding exasperated, though Bat didn't know why she'd expect him to know about a girlfriend. "Suzette. Remember? From the doughnut shop?"

"Dad said she was a friend," Bat said.

"That's what he *said*," replied Janie.

Bat looked at Dad. So did Janie.

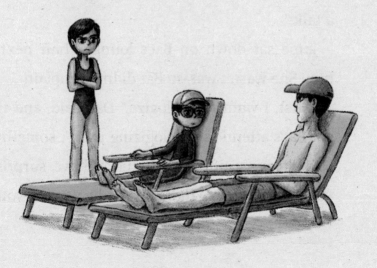

"Well," Dad said. But that was all he said.

"See?" said Janie, and she turned and marched toward the pool.

Dad stood up. "Wait," he called after Janie. "Come back!"

Janie stopped and stood, facing away from Bat and Dad, her arms crossed. Her whole body looked tense, and Bat could see how strong she'd gotten with all the swimming. Then she turned around and walked back.

"Sit down," Dad said, and he sat too. "Let's have a talk."

Janie sat down on Bat's lounge chair next to him. She wasn't wet, so Bat didn't complain.

"First, I want to apologize," Dad said, and that got Bat's attention. Apologizing wasn't something Dad did very often. "I shouldn't have surprised you guys the way I did. I just really wanted you to meet my friend Suzette. I went about it the wrong way. I promise not to do that again."

Next to Bat, Janie's shoulders softened. "I like surprises," she said. "Just not that surprise."

"I get it," Dad said. "And I'm sorry. Do you forgive me?"

"Yes," said Janie, but she didn't sound sure about it.

"How about you, Bat?"

"I wasn't mad at you," he answered.

Dad smiled. "Okay, sport," he said.

"But is Suzette your girlfriend or your friend?" Bat asked.

Dad adjusted his baseball cap lower over his eyes. It took him a little while to answer. "She's somewhere in between," he said finally. "More than a friend, but not really a girlfriend. Maybe she'll be my girlfriend eventually."

"What changes a friend into a girlfriend?" Bat asked. "Is it kissing?"

Now Dad looked uncomfortable. He took off his hat and squeezed it, put it on again. "Sometimes," he said.

Bat imagined his dad kissing Suzette, but it was hard for him to picture because he couldn't really remember what she looked like. He hadn't paid very good attention when he'd met her at the doughnut shop, because he'd been worried about Janie's headache. Next time they met, he promised himself, he'd pay better attention.

"I like our bike rides and going to the doughnut shop together," Bat said. "It's one of the best parts about Every-Other Weekends."

"Yeah," said Janie, and she smiled at Bat, a big, wide smile. "Me too. It's like our tradition. Just the three of us."

"Just the three of us," Dad said, and he nodded. "Okay. I'll remember that. Deal?" he said, and he offered his hand to Janie.

"Deal," she said, smiling at Dad now in that same open way, and they shook hands.

"Deal," said Bat, and he shook Dad's hand, and then Janie's hand, which made everyone laugh.

"Okay," Dad said again, and this time when he said it, it felt like they were starting over, in a good way. "How about we all go for a dip in the pool? What do you say?"

"Okay," Janie said, standing up.

"No face splashing," Bat said.

"No face splashing," promised Janie and Dad together.

CHAPTER 18
Photo Shoot

The following Friday was the hottest day of the summer. Inspired by Jenny and Babycakes, Bat put Thor in the bathtub. The skunk stretched out long, his belly pressing into the cool white enamel. He was the size of a small cat.

Janie and Bat sat on the cool tile floor, watching Thor and eating Popsicles. Janie's was grape; Bat's was orange.

When she'd taken the last bite of her Popsicle, Janie dropped the stick into the bathtub for Thor to sniff. It startled him a little, and he puffed up his tail.

"Careful," Bat warned. "You've got to move slowly."

Janie sat very still, and after a moment, Thor stretched out his twitchy nose to smell the stick, then lick it. His tail depuffed.

"I didn't mean to startle him," Janie said.

"Skunks are nearsighted," Bat told her. "He probably didn't notice the stick until it was right up next to him."

Thor lost interest with the Popsicle stick and wandered over to the bathtub drain. He poked at it with his nose for a minute, then plopped down and rolled over onto his back. Slowly, Bat reached his hand into the bathtub and scratched his belly.

"He's awfully tame," Janie said. "He reminds me of a cat."

"People think that skunks just go around spraying," Bat told her, "but actually they only spray when they are really scared, and they always warn you first."

Now Thor was stretching his arms up over his head so that Bat could scratch his furry little armpits.

"That's adorable," Janie said. "Hang on. Just a second."

She slid away from the edge of the bathtub and stood up slowly so as not to startle Thor. Bat could hear her walking down the hall to her room and then coming right back. She had her camera.

Bat stopped scratching Thor so that Janie could get a good picture of him, but she said, "No, scratch him some more! It makes him stretch out all cute and funny."

Bat obliged, and Thor arched his back in pleasure. Janie took a picture, then showed it to Bat. There was Thor, captured forever in his adorable pose, stretched out, with Bat's hand on his belly.

Then Janie said, "I have an idea. Let's do a photo shoot!"

"With Thor?" asked Bat.

"Yes," Janie answered.

"I don't know if he'd like that," Bat said.

"It'll be fun! And we'll be careful not to make him nervous," Janie said.

Bat looked at Thor, who was scratching at his ear with a back foot. The skunk was getting so big. Very soon, Bat knew, Mom would say it was time to let him go into the wild. It would be nice to have more pictures. "Okay," he said. "But we're not dressing him up in doll clothes or anything. That would be disrespectful."

Janie laughed. "Sometimes you say the funniest things, Bat."

Bat hadn't said it to be funny. "I'm serious," he said.

"I know," Janie said. "That's what makes it even funnier."

They decided that the best place to do the photo shoot would be in the kitchen.

"It has the best light," Janie said, "and lots of space."

Bat brought his beanbag chair into the kitchen, and Janie draped it with a blue-and-white checked tablecloth, making a nice little nest. Then Bat set Thor in it.

"Okay," Janie said, "you make him sit still, and I'll take the pictures."

"Thor isn't really the kind of animal you can

128

make do anything," Bat warned.

"Just try," Janie said, so Bat tried. He tried cooing Thor's name, soft and high, the way Thor liked to hear it. He tried waving his hands around behind Janie's head to get Thor's attention. He tried playing soothing music on the little radio that Mom kept next to the sink.

But Thor just kept snuffing around, scooting out of the beanbag chair and poking his way into the corners of the kitchen.

Janie kept taking pictures anyway, action shots of Thor maneuvering between chair legs and nudging around the trash can.

Then she said, "Let's get a few with the two of you together," so Bat gently picked Thor up and cradled him in his arms. Thor's black whiskers twitched eagerly toward Bat's face, and Bat leaned down to kiss his head.

Janie snapped a picture.

"Maybe sit with him in the beanbag," Janie suggested.

Bat sat down and crossed his legs, and then put Thor up on his shoulder the way he'd been doing lately. Thor crawled familiarly around the back of Bat's neck and flopped down like a collar. Bat turned his face toward Thor, and Thor stretched his nose toward Bat.

"Oh, that's adorable," Janie said, and she snapped another picture.

CHAPTER 19
Mail Day

///

Dear Bat,

Hello from Canada!

I hope you are having a good summer. I am having lots of fun! My cousin Robert lives near a lake, and we walk there every day to swim. The water is freezing! There is a floating dock way out far, and yesterday I swam all the way there without a kickboard for the first time. Robert is a really good swimmer. He can make it all the way across the lake, without a kickboard! And he's really tall. He's on his school's basketball team!

I met this kid named Marlo and I told him about you and Thor and he told me that his neighbor once tamed a little bird that fell out of a nest and he kept it all winter and then let it go the next spring, and the bird comes back every year now to visit! Maybe after you release Thor, he will come back to visit you too.

How is Thor? Is he getting big? I'll be home in ten days. I hope I'll get to see him again before you have to let him go.

What have you been doing this summer? Have you seen Babycakes at all? I wonder how she likes Jenny's house.

I hope you write back soon!

Your friend,
Israel

Bat sat at the kitchen table, and Thor was at his feet, nibbling at a little salad that Bat had made him for a snack.

Janie looked over from whatever she was doing on her computer and smiled at Thor eating his salad. She snapped a quick picture of the skunk and then went back to her work.

Bat had read the letter from Israel three times, and each time he finished it, he refolded it, tucked it back into its envelope, and admired the colorful stamps and the way his name and address looked printed in Israel's blocky handwriting: "BAT, 9 Plum Lane."

It was the first letter Bat had ever gotten in the mail. He'd gotten birthday cards from his family, and last summer before school started, Mr. Grayson had sent a welcome letter to all the kids who would be in his class. But this was different.

This was a letter from a friend.

Bat was happy that Israel had sent him a letter all the way from Canada. But he noticed that Israel didn't say anything about missing home. And he talked a lot about his cousin Robert. Maybe Israel was having such a good time that he would never want to come home. Maybe he was having such a good time that Robert would be his best friend now instead of Bat.

After he'd finished reading Israel's letter for the third time, Bat laid it out on the table and smoothed it flat. He stood up carefully, picking up Thor and balancing him on his shoulders, and went to his room to get a piece of paper and a pencil. Then he went back to the kitchen and sat down again, all without disturbing Thor, who was awake but perfectly relaxed. The soft, warm weight of the skunk resting on his shoulders helped Bat to feel calmer and less worried about whether Israel was missing home and whether he liked Robert more than Bat.

Janie, who was still sitting across the table from Bat with her laptop open in front of her, watched Bat sit down. "Wow," she said. "Thor sure likes it up there on your shoulders." She picked up her camera from where it rested on the table and took a picture of Bat and Thor.

Bat didn't say anything. He was focused on what he was going to write.

Dear Israel,

Thor is getting big. He's like a small cat now. He eats and sleeps a lot and is good about using his litter.

This summer I have been helping Laurence at my mom's veterinary clinic. I help with baths and walks and I hold the dog paws steady while Laurence clips their claws. Also, I have been riding bikes with my dad and Janie, and one day we went to the pool. It was hot.

I saw Babycakes when Jenny and her grandmother brought her into the vet clinic when she was sick and then at Jenny's house.

Your friend,

Bat

Bat read his letter through two times. It was shorter than Israel's letter to him.

"Janie," he said. "I need your help."

"What is it?" Janie asked, but she didn't look up from the computer. She was typing.

"Israel wrote me a letter and I wrote back, but his letter is way longer than mine."

"Just a second," Janie said, and she typed a little more, and then there was the whooshing sound of an email being sent, and then she closed the laptop. "Let me see," she said.

Bat passed her both letters, the longer one that

Israel had written and the shorter one that he had written in response.

"Well, Bat, all you did was answer his questions. That's why your letter is so short."

Bat had been careful to read closely through Israel's letter and to answer each question he'd asked. "That's what you're supposed to do when someone asks a question," Bat said. "You're supposed to answer it."

"Well, sure," said Janie, "but writing a letter to a friend isn't like taking a test. You don't have to *just* answer the questions. You're supposed to say more!"

Bat was irritated. He felt like chewing on the neck of his shirt, but Thor was comfortable on his shoulders and Bat didn't want to pull the shirt out from under him and make him slide off.

"What else am I supposed to say?" Bat asked.

"Look," Janie said. She took his pencil and lightly underlined some of the sentences in Israel's letter. "See?" she said. "All of this is just Israel telling you stuff about himself, his summer, stuff like that. You don't have any of that in your letter. You only answer his questions, and you don't give any extra information. Like here," she said, tapping the pencil on Bat's letter, where he wrote about Babycakes coming to the clinic. "You write that Babycakes was sick, but you don't say what happened, or that she got better, or anything! And also, you don't ask Israel anything about *his* summer. It's more thoughtful to ask some questions back."

Bat hadn't thought about it that way. "But," he said, "even if I *did* ask Israel questions, he wouldn't have time to answer them and send me another letter back. By the time I send this letter to Canada, and he gets it, and reads it, and writes another letter, and sends it to me, he'll be home already."

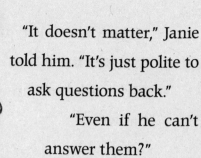

"It doesn't matter," Janie told him. "It's just polite to ask questions back."

"Even if he can't answer them?"

"Even if," Janie said, and she sounded sure. "Sometimes, it's nice to know that someone is wondering about you when you're not together."

So Bat erased the bottom part of his letter, where he had written, *Your friend, Bat,* and he wrote some more about how Babycakes had had the snuffles and head tilt, and how she'd had to stay at the vet clinic for four nights, but that she had taken antibiotics and she was all better.

Now Bat's letter was almost as long as Israel's.

"How many questions should I ask?" Bat said to Janie.

"I don't know, Bat, just a few," said Janie.

"A few is three," said Bat.

"Then ask him three," Janie said.

Bat wrote,

How is the weather in Canada?
Are you homesick?
When you get home, do you want to have another sleepover with me?

And then he rewrote,

Your friend,
Bat

Satisfied, he folded the letter into thirds. "Where do we keep envelopes?" he asked.

CHAPTER 20
A Hot, Sweaty Day

Sometimes, Bat had a hard day. If he had a hard day in Mr. Grayson's class, Bat would cuddle Babycakes, even if it was time for science or reading circle, thanks to Mr. Grayson's open-door Babycakes policy.

Wednesday was a hard day. Mom had the afternoon off work, but she had to spend the whole time running errands. Because Janie was at the pool again with some friends, Bat had to run the errands too.

The air-conditioning in the car was not working properly; all week, it had taken way too long for the car to cool. It was so hot that they had to roll down all four windows, which Bat hated because it made a really loud noise and it blew his hair all around.

"Put on your hat," Mom suggested, looking at Bat in the rearview mirror.

Bat took the baseball cap Dad had given him from the pocket in the back of Mom's seat and put it on. It helped with the hair but not with the sound.

And then there were the lines. Everywhere they went—the hardware store, the grocery store, the dry cleaners—it was waiting and waiting and more waiting.

And each time they came out of one place to drive to the next place, the car was even hotter. Bat's T-shirt stuck to his back with sweat. His socks felt too tight around his ankles. The hat was making his head itch, but when he took it off, the wind blew his hair and so he put it back on.

"I'm really sorry, Bat, but we have to make one more stop," Mom said as she checked her phone after they left the dry cleaners. "We just have to swing by the pool and pick up Janie."

"I thought she was getting a ride home with Ezra," Bat said. He knew his voice sounded whiny, but he couldn't make it sound different.

"That's what I thought too, but she sent me a message that she's ready to come home now," Mom said. She laid the dry cleaning in the back of the station wagon, next to the groceries and the bag with light bulbs and batteries from the hardware store. Bat groaned and climbed reluctantly into the back seat.

"Can't she walk home?"

"Bat," said Mom, "no. It's too far for her to walk."

"Then she should wait for Ezra's mom," Bat whined.

"I know you're frustrated and ready to go home," Mom said. "But we're going to pick her up. If you needed to come home from something early, Janie and I would pick you up. That's the way we do things."

So, after all those errands, they had to drive all the way across town to the pool. And in the meantime, Bat could practically *hear* the ice cream melting in the grocery bag.

And then, when they got to the pool, Janie wasn't even in the front waiting for them! They waited a whole extra five minutes before she came out to the parking lot. In those five minutes, Bat's head got so itchy from the hat that he had to take it off again.

"What took you so long?" Bat blurted when Janie got into the car at last.

"Jeez, Bat, don't yell," Janie said loudly.

"*You're* yelling," Bat yelled back.

"I'm not yelling," Janie said.

"You're not yelling *now*," Bat said. "You were yelling before."

"Whatever, Bat," Janie said, and she rolled her eyes and crossed her arms.

Which hurt his feelings. Bat crossed his arms too, but because it was so hot, that was uncomfortable, so he uncrossed them.

"Everything okay?" Mom asked Janie when they'd pulled out of the parking lot and onto the main road.

"No," said Janie.

"Do you want to talk about it?" Mom asked.

"No," said Janie again, but then, a minute later, she said, "Ezra always thinks he's so funny."

"Ah," Mom said.

"*I* don't think Ezra is always funny," said Bat. "Sometimes, he's a mean tease."

Janie sniffed. Mom looked at her in the rearview mirror. "Did Ezra tease you, Janie?" she asked.

"I don't want to talk about it," Janie said, but then, after the next red light, she said, "I don't think it's weird that I like to use my camera to take pictures instead of my cell phone. I don't think it makes me stuck-up!"

"Is that what Ezra said?" Mom asked.

Janie nodded.

"I don't think it's weird," Bat said. "I like your camera."

"That wasn't very nice of Ezra," Mom said.

"I don't want to talk about it," Janie said again.

"If you don't want to talk about it," Bat said, "then why do you keep talking about it?"

"*You're* not always nice either, Bat," said Janie.

"No one is *always* nice," Bat said. He didn't tell Janie that she had hurt his feelings. He just looked out his window.

The rest of the ride home was silent, except for the rush of air coming in through the windows, and when Mom pulled into the driveway and turned off the car, Janie jumped out and slammed her door.

"She slammed the door," Bat told Mom.

"I know, Bat," Mom said. She sighed and rubbed

the spot right above her nose. "I heard."

"We're not supposed to slam doors," Bat said.

"That is true," Mom said. "But sometimes, we slam them anyway."

Bat slid out of the back seat. His T-shirt felt glued to his back.

"Will you help me carry in the stuff from our errands?" Mom asked.

"Why doesn't Janie have to help?" Bat asked. He just wanted to go inside and change his shirt. He didn't want to be out in the hot sun for one more minute.

"Because Janie is having a hard day," Mom said.

"I'm having a hard day too!" said Bat. "My day has been harder than Janie's. I had to run errands and the air-conditioning is broken and then we had to drive all the way to the pool instead of home."

"Okay, Bat," Mom said. "We don't need to have

an argument about who has had the hardest day. I'll get the bags myself. You can go inside."

Bat went inside. He went to his room and took off his sweaty T-shirt and put on a clean one. But he didn't feel better. He felt worse, because part of him knew that he should have stayed outside to help his mom bring in all the errand stuff. But then he heard the front door close and he knew it was too late to go back out to help.

Bat just stood in the center of his room.

Then he heard a rustling sound. It was Thor, who was awake, and who had come out of his nest in the corner of his pen when he heard Bat. He pressed his nose between the panels of the enclosure.

"Hey, little Thor," Bat cooed. Even if it was a bad day, he wanted to use a good voice with the skunk. He opened the gate and Thor shuffled out. Bat admired how thick and bristly his tail was getting, how shiny and clear his eyes looked, and how plump and healthy his belly was.

Thor came right up to Bat and pushed Bat's leg with his snout. Bat crouched down and scooped him up and then walked over to his bed. He lay down on his side, facing the wall, and made a little crook with his arm to cradle the skunk.

For some reason that Bat couldn't name, he started to cry. Not a lot, but a little, and his body shook and tears rolled down his cheeks.

Thor sniffed Bat's ear, his cheek, his nose. Bat closed his eyes. Thor's whiskers tickled Bat's face. His rough tongue brushed against Bat's skin, licking at the tears. Slowly, Bat stopped crying.

Above Bat's head, the ceiling fan whirled around and around, circulating nice, cool air. His bed was soft and comfortable. When Bat's tears were dried, Thor turned in a little circle and tucked his head

into the bend of Bat's elbow. Drowsy and perfectly comfortable, Bat and the skunk fell asleep
together.

CHAPTER 21
Two Parts

///

"Bat! Where's Thor?"

Bat woke, drowsily, to the sound of Mom's voice from the doorway to his bedroom. He turned his head to see her standing there looking worriedly at Thor's open enclosure.

"Shh," Bat whispered, not wanting to disturb the skunk, still curled in his arms, the end of his tail tucked over his nose. "He's right here."

Mom came into the room and across to the bed, peering over Bat to see the sleeping skunk. "Oh," she said, "he's with you."

"We took a nap," Bat said. His arm was stiff and tingly from being in the same position for so long, but he didn't want to move it. "My arm is asleep," he said.

Mom sat down gently on the edge of the bed. She rested her hand on Bat's leg. "My arm used to fall asleep when I would hold you or Janie in the same position for too long," she said. "I never wanted to shift and take the chance of waking you up."

"I know what you mean," Bat said.

They stayed there together, Thor sleeping, Bat and his mom watching him, for a long time, as the sky outside the window changed from blue to dusky pink. Finally, Thor twitched his nose, stretched all four of his legs, and yawned, his pink tongue curling out from between two rows of fine white teeth.

Then Bat rolled over and sat up. "You had a long nap, little Thor," he cooed. Thor blinked open his eyes, and he looked perfectly content and happy to find himself in Bat's arms. "I was sad," Bat told his mom, "but Thor made me feel better."

Bat stood and carried Thor to the enclosure and set him down. The skunk meandered over to his litter box and used it, then went to his water bowl for a nice long drink.

As Thor drank, Bat went to the kitchen to get a scoop of the special food he and Mom had made a couple of days earlier, following a recipe Bat had found on the internet and with special supplements that Mom had ordered through the vet clinic. It was a smelly mix of ground turkey, brown rice, and egg, mixed together with the supplements. They kept it in a plastic container in the refrigerator.

Thor must have smelled his supper, because when Bat went back into his room, the skunk scurried over to his enclosure's gate and paced excitedly.

"Okay, okay," Bat said in his soothing voice. "Settle down." He set Thor's dish on the plastic placemat Mom had let him take into his room, opened the enclosure's gate, and watched as Thor dug into his meal.

Mom was still there, sitting on Bat's bed. "You look happy," she said.

Bat nodded. "It's satisfying to watch him eat," he said. "It's the best feeling."

Mom laughed. "That's how I always felt when you or Janie would finish a whole plate of food."

Bat didn't like to think about what would happen when Thor was returned to the wild. Sometimes he started to imagine it, and he'd picture Thor's black-and-white tail disappearing into a bush, and then his eyes would fill with tears and his heart would feel like it was made of sharp splinters. Then he would do whatever it took to get the image out of his mind. He would let himself chew on his shirt or he would rock back and forth or he would kick the wall by his door over and over again, not really hard, not hard enough to hurt the wall, just hard enough to make his toes sore so that he could think about the pain in his foot instead.

He pictured it again now—Thor disappearing from him—and he pulled the collar of his shirt into his mouth and began to rock back and forth.

Mom stood up from the bed and came over to Bat. She stood close to Bat, and she opened her arms, which was her way of saying that if he wanted a hug, she was there to hug him.

Part of Bat didn't want anyone to touch him. That part of him felt like it was fighting with the part of him that very much *did* want a hug.

"I love you, Bat," Mom said softly, and then the part of him that wanted the hug was stronger, and he stepped into her arms.

CHAPTER 22
Pancake Juggling

"It was such a great trip! My cousin Robert has chickens, so every morning we went out to the coop to collect eggs, and we could eat as many as we wanted. They were delicious! *Way* better than store-bought eggs. And their yolks were orange instead of yellow. And we went swimming every afternoon, and we slept in bunk beds, and my cousin Robert knew about a million jokes *and* he can juggle. You would have liked it."

Israel was home at last. He was darker from the sun and maybe taller, too. He had gotten home the day before, and the first thing Bat and Israel were going to do together was visit Babycakes at Jenny's house. Israel's dad, Tom, was driving them there, in his truck. Then later they would go back to Bat's house for a sleepover.

"What did he juggle, clubs or balls?" Bat asked. "Laurence can juggle clubs, too. Lots of people can."

"He can juggle anything!" Israel said enthusiastically. "Clubs, balls, toys, spoons—you name it, he can juggle it."

"Apples," Bat said.

"Yep," said Israel.

"Calculators," Bat said.

"Definitely," said Israel.

"Pancakes," said Bat.

"Pancakes?" said Israel.

"Yes," said Bat. "Pancakes."

Israel thought about that. "I don't know," he said. "Pancakes are pretty floppy. And sticky."

"I'm going to learn to juggle pancakes," Bat said, even though the thought of floppy, sticky pancakes in his hands made him uncomfortable.

"Okay," said Israel, and he grinned at Bat. He had a big, happy smile, and Bat loved it. He smiled back.

"Here we are," Tom announced, pulling up in front of Jenny's house. "Last stop!"

"This is the first stop," Bat said. "Later you're taking us to my house."

Tom turned around to look at Bat in the truck's narrow back seat. He smiled too. "We missed you, Bat," he said. Then he said, "Okay, I'm going to run to the grocery store, and I'll be back to pick you boys up in an hour."

Maybe Jenny had been watching from the front window, because she opened the door before Bat and Israel had gone all the way up the walkway. "Hi, Bat! Hi, Israel!" she said.

"Hi, Jenny," said Israel.

"Where is Babycakes?" asked Bat.

"She's in my room," Jenny said. "Come on in."

Bat and Israel followed Jenny into the house and down the hall to her bedroom.

"Did Bat tell you that Babycakes was sick?" Jenny asked Israel.

"Yes," said Israel. "How is she now?"

"She's great! We gave her all the antibiotics. Bat's mom is amazing. She even came to check on Babycakes here at our house."

Jenny's bedroom door was open. Bat could see Babycakes's hutch and the white fluffy shape of Babycakes inside it.

"Hey, Babycakes!" Israel said.

The bunny looked up. Her whiskers twitched as if she was saying hello. Her eyes were clear and bright. Her head was straight, not tilted at all anymore. She looked freshly brushed, and her food dish and water bottle were both full.

"Jenny," Bat said, "you are an excellent animal caretaker."

Jenny's face turned red. "Thank you, Bat," she said. "That means a lot, coming from you."

After they all petted Babycakes and told her what a good fluffy bunny she was, Bat and Israel and Jenny went into the kitchen and drank the orange juice her mom had poured for them and ate some cookies. They were not as good as the cookies Janie made at home, but Bat didn't say that out loud, even though it was true.

Then Jenny asked Israel, "How was your trip to Canada?"

And Bat had to listen again as Israel told Jenny all the stuff he'd already told Bat—about the chickens, and the swimming, and Robert's amazing juggling.

"My cousin Robert is really cool," Israel told Jenny. "He's probably going to come visit me next spring. His parents say they can put him on a plane all by himself and we can pick him up from the airport and he can stay for a whole week!"

"Is he your best friend now?" Bat said. He hadn't meant to say that out loud, and as soon as he did, he wished he could pull the words back into his mouth.

"What?" said Israel.

"Nothing," said Bat. "Never mind."

"Ba-at," said Israel. "Robert is my cousin and he's cool and he can juggle anything—well, *almost* anything—but you're my best friend."

Bat smiled. "I'm glad you're home," he told Israel.

"Me too," Israel answered. "Even though I'm going to miss those eggs."

When Bat and Israel were back in Tom's truck, driving to Bat's house for their sleepover, Israel said, "Bat, I want to ask you something. But promise not to get mad, okay?"

"I can't promise not to get mad," Bat said. "I don't know what you're going to ask."

Israel blew out of his mouth, making a sound like a deflating balloon. Then he glanced up at his dad, who was looking at them in the rearview mirror. Tom smiled a little, which seemed to encourage Israel to speak. "Well, try not to *act* mad. Like, don't yell or say anything mean."

Bat nodded. He couldn't help his feelings, but he could try to help how he reacted. Like when he was around Thor—then, even if Bat had big uncomfortable feelings, he tried to remember not to make scary loud sounds or move too quickly, because if he did, Thor might spray. Bat could make the sounds and move his body around, but not in the same room as Thor. "I'll try," Bat promised.

"It's about your skunk," Israel said. "I'm worried

about what's going to happen when you let him go."

Bat didn't like thinking about releasing Thor into the wild, and he didn't like talking about it, either. But he remembered how it had felt to talk about it with Jenny, that day in her bathroom. It hadn't felt good. But maybe it felt better than *not* talking about it.

"I'm worried too," Bat said at last. "I don't know how he is going to find food, or if he will know how to find a dry place to sleep when it rains." Prickly tears filled his eyes.

"Oh," said Israel. "I didn't even think about those things."

"Bat," said Tom from the driver's seat as they pulled up to a red light, "Israel is worried about *you.*"

"About me?" Bat asked.

"Yeah," said Israel. "About *you*."

Israel was worried about *him*. The ache in Bat's chest that came from worrying about Thor felt a little bit better, knowing that Israel was worried about him. Not all the way better. But a little better.

"Are you going to be okay?" Israel asked.

It took Bat a long time to answer, because his throat felt too tight for words to get through. When he did talk, his voice cracked and hurt. "I'm going to be really, really sad," he finally said.

Israel sighed and dropped his arm around Bat's shoulders. "Me too," he said.

Tom looked at them in the rearview mirror. "Me three," he said. The three of them sat quietly in the cab of the truck, engine rumbling.

Then the light turned green, and they started on their way again.

CHAPTER 23
Family Meeting

//

"Hey, Bat, isn't that your dad's car?" Israel asked when Tom pulled his truck up to the front of Bat's house.

Yes—that was Dad's little yellow sports car, parked in the driveway next to Mom's burgundy wagon.

"It's not an Every-Other Weekend," Bat said. "He only comes over on Every-Other Weekends."

Israel followed Bat up to the front door. It was unlocked. Bat pushed the door open.

"Mom?" he said.

"We're in here," said Mom from the kitchen.

Israel trailing behind, Bat went into the kitchen.

There was his mom, and his dad, and Janie, all sitting at the table. Janie had her laptop closed in front of her.

"Hey, sport!" Dad said.

"Bat," said Mom, "your dad dropped by because he wanted to talk about something. And I agree. It's time we have a family meeting. About Thor."

"Maybe I should go, Bat," Israel said. "We can do the sleepover another night."

"No," said Bat. "Stay. You're my best friend."

"Please stay," Bat's mom said, so Israel did.

They all sat around the kitchen table, Bat's dad sitting on the kitchen stool because there weren't enough chairs for everyone.

They were going to tell him that it was time to release Thor. Bat was sure that was what they were going to say. But it wasn't the right thing to do. Bat felt certain about that. He and Thor belonged together. And he wasn't going to let Thor go without a fight.

"I don't want to let Thor go into the wild," Bat said. It felt so good to say the words out loud, the words he had been thinking all summer. "I want to keep him forever. I am the best skunk caretaker for Thor, and he belongs with me." Bat folded his arms across his chest, ready to fight with everyone.

"I agree," said Israel, even though he wasn't family and this was a family meeting. "Bat loves Thor, and Thor loves Bat."

Bat smiled at Israel. He was so glad his friend was home from Canada, and he was glad that

Israel was on his side. Israel smiled back, with all his teeth.

"You are a good friend, Israel," Bat's mom said.

"Thank you," said Israel. "Bat is a good friend too."

It felt good to know that at least Israel agreed with him. And then Janie spoke.

"I think Bat should keep Thor too," she said.

"Really?" said Bat. His arms loosened in surprise. It was true that Janie had gotten nicer about the skunk since the night Thor sprayed at her school play. She had given Thor a hairbrush, and she'd taken pictures of him, and she'd sometimes visited Thor in Bat's room. But Bat would never have guessed that Janie would want Thor to stay.

"Yes," said Janie. She opened her laptop and pressed a few keys. "Look," she said, and then she turned the laptop around so that everyone else could see it. "Remember Dr. Jerry Dragoo, the skunk expert Bat wrote to when we first rescued Thor?"

Dr. Jerry Dragoo was the founder of the Dragoo Institute for the Betterment of Skunks and Skunk Reputations, and he had told Bat that even though skunks don't usually make good pets, what makes a good pet is a good caretaker. And that had made Bat determined to be the best possible caretaker for Thor.

"Well," said Janie, "I wrote to him. I sent him a bunch of pictures of Bat and Thor that I've taken over the summer. See?"

And there were the pictures—Thor on Bat's lap, his eyes closed in pleasure as Bat groomed him with Janie's hairbrush; Thor eating a meal that Bat had prepared; the vegetable garden Israel and Bat had planted, green and full, with the little painted sign that read "Thor's Garden"; Bat with Thor draped across his shoulders, their noses touching.

"I told Dr. Jerry Dragoo how much you love Thor, and what a good caretaker you are," Janie said. "I told him how gentle and kind you are with him, and how you stay calm around him, even when it's hard for you. I told him that Thor has only gotten scared enough to spray that one time. And Dr. Jerry Dragoo wrote back to me."

"Read us the email he sent, Janie," said Dad.

Janie turned the laptop back around and read.

"'Dear Janie,'" she began. "'Thank you for sending the pictures of Bat and Thor. It is clear that Bat is an excellent caretaker, and that he and Thor are very attached to each other. It is almost always best for a skunk to be returned to the wild, but in a situation such as this, when the skunk has bonded to his caretaker and when the caretaker has bonded to his skunk, the best decision for both boy and skunk would be for them to remain together. Bat and Thor are very lucky to have each other, and Bat is also very lucky to have a sister like you.'"

Janie looked up from her laptop, grinning.

Bat could hardly believe it. "Is that why you took all those pictures?" he asked.

"Yes," said Janie. "For evidence."

To Bat, love meant doing things. Bat showed Thor how much he loved him by feeding him and cleaning his litter box and grooming his coat. And right then, sitting in the kitchen, Bat felt more certain than he ever had that Janie loved him. Because of what she had done for him and Thor. Because of evidence.

"That's so cool that you wrote to Dr. Jerry Dragoo, and he wrote back!" Israel said.

"Thanks," said Janie. She closed her laptop.

Bat's dad said, "You might not believe this, but *I* wrote to a skunk expert too. And today I got his response. That's why I stopped by." He pulled a folded-up letter from his pocket. "I was telling my friend Suzette about Thor, and she mentioned that she'd once met a scientist who studies skunks. Get this—his name is Dr. Ted Stankowich!"

"Stankowich?" said Israel. "That's the perfect name for a skunk expert!"

"What did Dr. Stankowich say?" Bat asked.

"He says that a skunk as bonded as Thor is to you probably wouldn't do very well in the wild," Dad said. "He might be too friendly with humans, who could think he's dangerous if he walked right up to them, and he might not know how to deal with predators, like coyotes or owls. And then, at the end, he wrote, 'Skunks that are bonded to owners make terrific, loving pets if raised in the right way.'" Dad looked up from the letter and smiled. "And you've certainly raised Thor well," he said. "I'm really proud of how good you are with him."

Bat smiled back. His dad wasn't a fan of animals, like Bat and Mom were. But still, he'd written to Dr. Stankowich, and he thought that Bat should keep Thor too. "That's cool that you found another skunk expert," Bat said. "Thank you."

Dad grinned. "I love you, sport."

And this time, the nickname didn't bother Bat at all.

Mom cleared her throat. "I've been doing some research too," she said. "And, Bat, I agree with Dr. Jerry Dragoo, and Dr. Stankowich, and your dad, and your sister, and Israel. You and Thor belong together."

Bat could hardly believe what he was hearing. He didn't have to fight at all. Everyone understood how much he and Thor needed each other.

They understood. They understood *him*.

Bat looked around at all the smiling faces. Mom, and Dad, and Janie, and Israel. Light was coming through the kitchen window, shining in golden dapples on everyone.

His body felt all sorts of things mixed up together—happy and excited and sort of sick, like he'd been on a roller coaster. Overwhelmed, like he needed to be alone for a while, and grateful, like he wanted to stay right where he was. He felt his elbows bend and his hands beginning to flap, which helped him to feel better.

"I'll be right back," Bat said at last. He stood up and went to his room. For a minute, he just stood there as his hands calmed down and dropped to his sides, as he breathed deeply until his stomach stopped fluttering. There were tears on his cheeks, Bat realized, and he wiped them away. He took one more deep, ragged breath. Then he walked over to the enclosure, where Thor was curled into a ball in his T-shirt nest.

Bat opened the gate. "Little Thor," he cooed softly. Thor blinked open his eyes, yawned lazily, and stretched. Then he walked right over and waited to be picked up. Bat scooped up the skunk gently, held him close, and kissed his head. Thor nuzzled his leathery nose into the crook of Bat's neck, just the way he always did.

"Come on," Bat said, helping Thor onto his favorite spot, Bat's shoulder. "We're having a family meeting."

Bat walked back to the kitchen, Thor balanced on his shoulder. Everyone was still there, at the table, waiting for him.

"We're back," Bat said. "We're all here now. The whole family."

The kitchen was full of sunlight, and love, and warmth. It was full with a mom who was a hero veterinarian, and a dad who was trying to do better every day, and a good sister who sometimes had hard days too, just like Bat, and a best friend, home from Canada, and a perfect skunk named Thor, and a boy called Bat, who knew, right then, that he was exactly where he belonged.

Author's Note

Believe it or not, not only is there a real Dr. Jerry Dragoo, who really does run the Dragoo Institute for the Betterment of Skunks and Skunk Reputations, there is *also* a real Dr. Ted Stankowich!

Both of these experts agree that the best place for wild animals is in the wild . . . except in a rare case like Thor's, when the animal is so bonded to humans that being released wouldn't be safe.

You can visit Dr. Jerry Dragoo's website at

www.dragoo.org and the Stankowich Lab at www
.csulb.edu/~tstankow if you'd like to learn more.

Heartfelt thanks to Dr. Jerry Dragoo and Dr.
Ted Stankowich for their input and advice.

Acknowledgments

//

Writing Bat's story has been a unique pleasure. I am so grateful to all the people who have joined me along Bat's journey: my friend Adah Nuchi; my agent, Rubin Pfeffer; my editor, Jordan Brown; all the wonderful people at Walden Pond Press— go, Team Bat!; real-life skunk experts Dr. Jerry Dragoo and Dr. Ted Stankowich; my own loving family; and the teachers, librarians, parents, and kids who love Bat, too.

In these books, Bat's circle of friendship and support grows and grows, and in writing and sharing these books, my own circle has grown, as well. Most of all, I'm grateful to Bixby Alexander Tam, the boy called Bat, for coming to me in the first place.

More Must-Read Books from Walden Pond Press

Also available as ebooks.